1 MONTH OF
FREE
READING

at

www.ForgottenBooks.com

By purchasing this book you are eligible for one month membership to ForgottenBooks.com, giving you unlimited access to our entire collection of over 1,000,000 titles via our web site and mobile apps.

To claim your free month visit:

www.forgottenbooks.com/free672379

ISBN 978-0-483-68821-6
PIBN 10672379

ANNA,

OR,

MEMOIRS OF A WELCH HEIRESS.

By MRS. _Agnes Maria_ BENNETT,

AUTHOR OF

ELLEN COUNTESS OF CASTLE HOWELL,

&c. &c.

FOURTH EDITION.

IN FOUR VOLUMES.

VOL. II.

LONDON:

PRINTED FOR WILLIAM LANE,

AT THE

Minerva-press,

LEADENHALL-STREET.

M.DCC.XCVI.

A N N A.

CHAPTER XXIII.

Grateful Pride.

WHEN Anna was firſt introduced at Dennis Place, Lady Edwin received her as a pretty country girl, who, merely from a dearth of more eligible companions, had been favoured with the notice of Mrs. Herbert; and her daughter Miſs Edwin not being uſed to exaggerate the charms or merit of her female acquaintance, had mentioned her in that light to her mamma; adding, ſhe was very good natured, and ſo great a favourite with Patty, it would be cruel to ſeparate them.

A   A hint

A hint was always fufficient to induce
Lady Edwin to adopt any mode confiftent
with her own ideas of propriety, that
would contribute to the happinefs of
another, particularly when that other was
the niece and great favourite of her hufband; fhe therefore confented to the invitation—and however obfcure Anna was in
other refpects, when fhe became a gueft
at Dennis Place, the owners confidered
her as entitled to every kind of refpect
and politenefs. But Lady Cecilia not
being interefted about her either by curiofity, benevolence or pride, fome days
had elapfed before fhe was familiar even
with the features of her face.

That intelligent index to a perfect foul
was not formed long to be overlooked,
the fweetnefs and delicacy of her animated
countenance at length called forth the admiration of Lady Cecilia, and rendered
the thoufand graces of her perfon and
converfation the more pleafing from their
having been fo long unobferved. Her
beau-

beautiful figure now ſtruck her Ladyſhip as embelliſhed with uncommon mental per-fections; ſhe was aſtoniſhed to find, tho' young and wholly ignorant of the world, her education and accompliſhments, added to a fine underſtanding and elegant man-ners, were equal to any thing ſhe had ever met in the firſt circles; they were indeed ſuch as claimed, and were honoured with every flattering mark of diſtinction, and in a ſhort time ſhe became the favourite companion of Lady Edwin.

Anna, ever obliging and grateful, ſtu-died the wiſhes of a lady who had not won leſs on her reſpect than affection, and per-ceiving as the ſtiff Trevanion hauteur wore off, the many great and good qualities that adorned the elevated rank of Lady Edwin, delighted in her ſociety. She was laughed at by Miſs Edwin for her ſtupid taſte:. but that young lady had a great deal more of her love than eſteem, venturing to think herſelf right, when perhaps Miſs Edwin conceived her wrong, ſhe was not to be laughed

A 2   out

out of a conduct that produced pleasure and improvement.

In one of the frequent airings, when Anna was honoured with a feat in Lady Edwin's cabriole, her noble conductress pointed out to her the beauty of the shrubs and flowers that grew in profusion on the wild mountain tops; adding, she would give the world to have the coat and train of a birth-day suit worked from them.

Embroidering was the forte of our heroine: Mrs. Manfel was one of the finest work-women in England, and being fond of the occupation had rendered her pupil equal to herself. Eager to cultivate the farther good will of Lady Cecilia, Anna instantly offered to finish one, by the Queen's birth-day, when Miss Edwin was to be presented.

Lady Edwin smiled at her eagerness to undertake a task which she did not believe could be accomplished, till she beheld the pencil of her young companion

tracing

tracing from life, in a very mafterly manner, the fhrubs fhe admired.

A piece of rich white fatin was directly written for, and from a temple, on the top of an adjacent hill, which ferved as a point of view from Dennis Place, the pattern was drawn and coloured with fuch tafte, that the fair artift began to be fpoken of as a prodigy at Dennis Place, while fhe was toafted by all the male vifitors round the country, as the lovelieft creature in it.

A month, the period allowed for this vifit, had paffed rapidly; another was preffingly requefted, but the fame letter that brought confent, gave Anna the fincereft grief, Mrs. Manfel had been feized with a fudden giddinefs in her head, which occafioned her falling down a ftone flight of fteps, and her indifpofition increafing with the lamenefs got by the fall, fhe had left Llandore Caftle.

Dennis Place, its grandeur, its elegance, its beauty; the flattering diftinction of Lady Edwin, the good humoured freedom of Sir William, nor the fociety of her

young

young friends, had now the leaft attraction for Anna; it was in vain they attempted to detain her! Mrs. Manfel, her dear maternal friend! her more than mother! was ill, and Lady Edwin was prevailed upon with great reluctance to fend her home, although her efteem was increafed by the motive by which fhe was actuated.

Anna found Mrs. Manfel much worfe than from Mrs. Herbert's reprefentation fhe expected, and the good, the worthy rector, almoft broken hearted; but her prefence diffufed joy in the bofoms of both her friends; Mrs. Manfel wept at fo lively an inftance of her affection, and faid fhe fhould now want no other doctor; and her hufband, whofe happinefs all centered in his wife, was in tranfpotts at the happy effect the fight of Anna produced. Slow and uncertain was that good woman's recovery; her leg, fwelled and inflamed, confined her at home; and her other complaints feldom permitted an intercourfe with her friendly neighbours.

This

This little abfence, tho' it had opened a new world to Anna, by introducing her to fcenes of fplendour as fuperior to any thing fhe had feen at Melmoth Lodge, as Melmoth Lodge was to the Parfonage, had the effect only of endearing to her thofe friends it had parted her from, and that peace fhe had left.

She was now arrived at an age, when the advantage of Mr. Melmoth's goodnefs to her became confpicuous in the fenfe and judgment, far beyond her years, which was exhibited in all her actions; the leffons fhe had received from him were thofe of purity and honour; fhe was early taught to hold vice, whatever fhape it might affume, in the moft perfect abhorrence. Thofe precepts were induftrioufly inculcated by her governefs, and enforced by the natural goodnefs of her own heart. An entire ftranger to deceit, fhe did net fufpect in others, what fhe had no idea of practifing; fhe had a great fhare of pride, which often rendered the fenfe of her dependant fituation on the charity

of

of ftrangers, infupportable, and that pride
firft pointed out the neceffity of employing thofe talents to advantage which
God had bleffed her with; fhe knew
the magnificence of Lady Edwin's fpirit,
and flattered herfelf, if the work pleafed,
which fhe had brought home, it would
prevent her being entirely a burthen on the
generofity of her friends, whofe income,
now in an expenfive illnefs, fhe feared muft
be little enough for themfelves; gladly
then fhe began a tafk on which fo much
depended, and as fhe chiefly fat by the
bed or eafy chair of her dear governefs,
fhe had the conftant benefit of advice and
inftruction in arranging the foil, and
fhading the flowers.

As foon as one breadth was finifhed, it
was fent to Dennis Place; Lady Edwin
was in raptures, and returned it with a
purfe of twenty pounds, which fhe begged
Anna would accept to purchafe for herfelf, if that was poffible, what would be
as pleafing to her as her work was to
Lady Edwin.

With

With equal joy and pride did Anna carry this purse to her invaluable friends; it would enable her, she told them, to look at them without confusion, if she might but hope she should ever be able to shew them the gratitude of her heart independent of her obligations; will, said the grateful girl, (throwing herself on her knees at their feet, the purse in her offering hands) will it be ever my happy lot to administer to your comforts? wants, I trust, you will have none, but, is it not possible your Anna may yet live to bless her dear governess?

If the reader has ever feasted on the sensibility of generous minds, he will, perhaps have some idea of the returns made by our Welsh parson and his wife, to the grateful overflowings of an uncorrupted heart; if he has not, description will do nothing for him; Mrs. Mansel slept not till she had sent for linen, a new riding habit, and other articles of rural finery, for our heroine *(all this any body may understand)* to the full amount of the twenty pounds.

CHAP.

CHAPTER XXIV.

Love in a Village.

BUT, anxious as Anna was to complete her tafk, and lame as Mrs. Manfel ftill continued, they were not entirely excluded from fociety; Mrs. Herbert vifited them conftantly, and fometimes ordered her cook to the parfonage with game, or any other little delicacy fhe hoped the invalid might like, and dined with them to tempt her to eat. In one of thofe vifitations, as fhe called them, a young man accompanied her, who had often met with Mr. and Mrs. Manfel at Llandore, but having been in England fome time on bufinefs, never happened to have feen Anna.

Mr. Wilkinfon had been employed in the Iron works, I have before mentioned,

as

as partly the property of Mr. Herbert, who engaged him from London for the purpose of over-looking and directing the Works; and he had so recommended him-self to the company by his knowledge, ingenuity, and industry, that he was admitted a partner, and allowed his share of the profits, instead of a salary, on condition of his living on the spot, and taking on him the attentive-part of the business.

Mrs. Herbert was very partial to Wilkinson; she was still more so to Anna; his prospects were great, her's were indifferent; but the amiable qualities of her mind, and the charms of her person were she thought, equivalent, and she had already made in her own ideas a match between this deserving pair. Without telling him any thing of her intention, he was invited to go to the parsonage to see a curious piece of work, but the lovely artist was not named. What she foresaw, came to pass, as far as related to Wilkinson: he fell desperately in love: but if he was charm-ed with Anna's person, what became of him when, drawn out by Mrs. Herbert, he heard her deliver, with equal wisdom and propriety, the sentiments of reason and rectitude, graced with the most enchanting vivacity, and when she was called upon to play and sing? Mrs. Herbert was one of the most valuable of women; she was not only extremely amiable in her manners, but of a sincere and friendly disposition; it was not therefore possible to refuse her request; and the wish to entertain in a manner most pleasing to herself, so kind a visitor, rendered Anna's performance worthy the friends whose partial commendations were always the height of her ambition.

Mr. Wilkinson, whose education had been far inferior to the strong natural parts he was blessed with, felt his passion for Anna, which increased every moment, with a fear, that so lovely, so accomplished a creature was not destined for him, while the object of his admiration sat wholly unconscious of Mrs. Herbert's design, or the power of her own charms, neither

suspecting

suspecting the one, or interested in the effect of the other.

When Mrs. Herbert and Mr. Wilkin-
son left the village, that lady soon induced
him, who was really enamoured, to declare
the state of his mind, and in return informed him of all she knew concerning Anna,
videlicit, that she was an orphan relation of
the Mansels; that her person and accomplishments were the whole of her fortune;
and that it would be, she supposed, a desir-
able thing with her friends, to marry her
to an honest man of good views; adding,
she thought *be* was that man, and as far as
she, who was partial to both, could judge,
there was a very fair prospect of happiness
in their union.

The result of this conversation was
Wilkinson's frequent visits to the parsonage, and soon after a declaration of his
sentiments to the rector, who declined,
according to a very foolish custom of his,
returning any answer till he had consult-
ed his wife; and Mrs. Mansel, on her
part, chose to make Anna acquainted
with

with her conqueſt, and to hear her ſentiments before ſhe communicated her
own.

The ſurpriſe and confuſion of our heroine at this addreſs was purely the effect
of innate modeſty; untinctured by the
leaſt atom of inclination for Wilkinſon,
or any other perſon, ſhe had not conſidered herſelf as the object of his attention,
nor had obſerved him with one jot more
curioſity than ſhe would have done his
grandfather; and ſo far from a partiality
towards him, or indeed, any of the ſex,
the idea of being particularly noticed,
gave her diſguſt rather than pleaſure; and
ſhe told her friends cooly, ſhe was too happy in their protection to wiſh it changed.

A negative ſo truly feminine, to a pro-
poſal of ſuch advantage, pleaſed Mr. Manſel; he congratulated her on her conqueſt,
of a man whoſe character, as well as circumſtances, were without doubt unob-
jectionable; and ſaid he hoped he ſhould
have the happineſs of giving his dear child

to

to a worthy young man who would be fenfible of fo great a bleffing.

This kind of language aftonifhed Anna,
fhe had no idea, fo fimple and fo frank
were her principles, that what fhe really
meant as a pofitive rejection, could be
miftaken, apparently alarmed and hurt at
Mr. Manfel's mifconftruction, fhe begged
not to be urged on the fubject; for fhe
was fure it was impoffible fhe could
ever feel the fentiments for Mr. Wilkinfon, fhe knew Mrs. Manfel felt for *him*,
and burfting into tears, expreffed her
fears, that this lady and her hufband
were weary of her,—tenderly embracing
her; they bid her not afflict herfelf; if,
faid Mrs. Manfel, he were an emperor, I
would not urge my Anna to any act, not
fanctified with her own full choice.

Her youth and inexperience were, to
thofe worthy people, fufficient reafons
for the averfenefs of Anna to the propofal
of the young man; but as they were fure
her affections were not engaged, they made
him happy, by the hope, that time might

crown

crown his wifhes with fuccefs; as they knew her heart free from any other impreffions, they advifed him to pay court to her efteem, fometime before he preffed for her hand, and gave him a general invitation to the houfe for that purpofe; he was treated with every mark of refpect and friendfhip by the rector and his lady, whofe health becoming every day more precarious, rendered this little addition to their fociety agreeable and entertaining, particularly as Mifs Herbert returned no more that fummer to Llandore, but was joined by her mother at Dennis Place.

As the long evenings approached, Mr. Wilkinfon took his abode at Llandore Caftle, the Works where he had a houfe, being at too great a diftance to go to, after fpending his evenings, as he conftantly did, at the parfonage.

He read to Anna whilft fhe fat at her frame, played a focial pool with Mr. and Mrs. Manfel at home, and when they mixed, which could be but feldom, in the diverfions, diverſions, that the guileleſs inhabitants of the place contrived not to kill, but for the enjoyment of time, he was always of the party; if they danced he was her partner; if ſhe rode out, he was her eſcort; and when ſhe walked, her companion; but thoſe interviews and conſtant opportunities, whilſt it riveted her conqueſt over Wilkinſon, did nothing for him; on the contrary, the more they were together, the leſs ſhe found herſelf inclined to favour his ſuit.

Mr. Wilkinſon was certainly a handſome, agreeable man, had ſomething peculiarly ſweet in his voice and addreſs, very genteel in his perſon, far above mediocrity in underſtanding, and at that time about eight or nine and twenty, he was therefore very unexceptionable in perſonal and mental accompliſhments, and his circumſtances now very good, were, by his great induſtry and care, every day enlarging; but to a heart like Anna's whoſe knowledge of mankind was merely theoretic, and ſomething more was wanting

ing; her own fentiments were the pure
effufions of innocence and virtue; Wilkinfon's might be no lefs, fo but he had
not that tender, delicate manner of expreffing them, that appeared neceffary to her
happinefs, and when, after a thoufand
fruitlefs attempts to fpeak, (wherein a
true lover, whofe paffion is unaffured of
fuccefs, always appears to difadvantage,)
he difclofed in faultering accents the
ftrong and refpectful affection he bore her,
he had the mortification of hearing from
lips unaccuftomed to deviate from truth,
and unacquainted with thofe artifices deceit in one fex renders neceffary in the
other, a firm and cool refufal of his offers;
his grief is not to be expreffed.

With a full heart and dejected countenance he repaired to the ftudy of Mr.
Manfel, whofe difappointment, the effect
of his affection for Anna, at this fteady
perfeverance in her firft declaration, was
almoft as great as the lover's; Mrs.
Manfel, however, declined, and requefted the fame forbearance from the

rector, interfering in a matter on which the happiness of her dear young friend so materially depended, and it was in vain that the enamoured Wilkinson intreated her interest; all he could obtain was, to continue his present footing in the family, an advantage he made the most of, being seldom absent, and taking care to favour the report of his being actually engaged to Miss Mansel, which, from their being always seen together, was universally believed.

CHAP.

CHAPTER XXV.

A New Acquaintance.

ON the laſt day of the year Lady Edwin's ſatin was taken out of the frame, and ſent to London; the encomiums beſtowed, by the beſt judges, on the work of Anna, was not more flattering to her pride, than the preſent that accompanied them, was to the grateful feelings of her heart. Mrs. Manſel accepted the office of her Banker, and a new piece of work was directly ſet about for Miſs Edwin.

Early in the ſpring, Mrs. Herbert's family returned to Wales; Anna, in her eighteenth year, and Miſs Herbert in her twentieth, had now formed the eſtabliſhment of a friendſhip no leſs laſting than ſincere; the girliſh amuſements they had

before

before adopted, were given up for more noble and useful pursuits.

The foundation of sense and taste, first laid by Mr. Melmoth, and carefully improved by Mrs. Mansel, was rapidly increasing to perfection in the mind of Anna; and those two ladies, both of the best dispositions, were of mutual benefit to each other.

Miss Herbert's education had been liberal, though not expensive; and Bath, where they spent so considerable a part of the year, gave her an acquaintance with the great world, of which our heroine was perfectly ignorant.

On the other hand, Anna, in her uninformed state, possessed a fund of book-knowledge; her sentiments were all the offspring of those impressions which her early advantages had engraved on her mind; with constant reading, she had happily blended great taste and judgment; she was blessed with a retentive memory; and the sort of things she chose to entertain her friend with in return for her lessons on polite life, were of a nature to be very well received by a sensible young woman; in fine they were quite satisfied with each other, and so fond of being together, that Mrs. Herbert consented Patty should spend one week at the parsonage, on condition Mrs. Mansel would spare Anna the other at Llandore.

In this friendly intercourse, without a single anxious thought to interrupt the serenity of the passing hour, except Mrs. Mansel's health, which then wore a more flattering aspect than it had lately done, was spent May, June, and July.

At this period, a young stranger to Anna made his appearance at Llandore; Mr. Charles Herbert and our heroine were perfectly acquainted with each other's character, and were mutually prejudiced by the descriptions they had heard; but high as his expectations were raised, the young student could not conceal his surprise, when his sister introduced him to her friend; to him she indeed appeared,

More

More than painting can exprefs,
Or youthful poets fancy when they love.

It was happy for him that his mother had fore-armed him with the intelligence (fhe believed true) of her being engaged to Wilkinfon, and that his notions of honour were of the old Cambrian ftamp, which forbad his invading the facred right of another.

Mr. Herbert was at this time in his twenty-fourth year; he had a very fine figure, and poffeffed an open, honeft, manly countenance : his eyes, when affected, fpoke to the heart, his teeth fine, and addrefs pleafing.

He was one of the braveft, yet moft compaffionate of men; at the inftant that a fenfe of injury roufed the lion in his foul, a tale of woe melted him to what is called womanifh weaknefs.

His purfe was open to the calls of the needy; he was too generous to be rich, and too fincere to be reckoned a faint.

Indeed fome little irregularities in the female line rendered Mrs. Herbert uneafy, left he fhould inherit his father's indifcretion,

tion ; but every doubt of his conduct vanifhed when fhe faw him.

He was the moft dutiful and affection-ate fon in the world; and his mother, in his opinion, the firft woman in it.

He was paffionate, the fault perhaps of his blood, but forgiving.

He was frank to a degree, fome people would fay of imprudence; but it was the franknefs of an honeft heart, which having in it nothing to hide, cared not who faw into its inmoft receffes.

To fay the thing that was not, was, in his eftimation, the moft contemptible of all vices; and to affect what he felt not, the moft difficult of all tafks.

The profeffion he was defigned for, obliged him to apply much to ftudy, but nothing was farther from him than pedantry; he was doted on by his parents; Mr. Herbert was proud and fond of him, and Patty and him appeared to have but one heart between them.

Such as he was, the firft interview con-vinced Anna there were men, and this

one

one of them, much nearer to her standard of perfection than Wilkinson, who was pre-sent, and did not, in her secret comparison, appear to the advantage he certainly wished.

What escapes the eye of love? the ad-miration of Herbert, as he examined the faultless countenance of Miss Mansel, the attention with which he regarded her every act, and the approbation visible in his tale-telling eyes when she spoke, conveyed a thousand fears into the bosom of poor Wil-kinson; jealousy, for the first time, found a place in his imagination; if, when the object he adored saw only him, or received not the least attention from any man but himself, she preserved her coldness and de-clined his love, what had he now to fear, when an amiable and accomplished rival might be ready to seize every advantage her indifference to him could give.

One only means struck him to avert the dreadful blow; he knew the honour, the probity of young Herbert's principles, he was sure he could not be guilty of in-juring him, if once he conceived Anna his

affianced right; their engagement, he
knew, would be fecurity againſt any attempts to fuperfede him in her affections;
and this artifice, the firſt he had ever been
guilty of, he put in practice the moment
an opportunity -offered; he gravely and
roundly afferting his engagement, which
being innocently corroborated by Mrs.
Herbert, and believed by every body in
the neighbourhood, admitted not a doubt
with Charles Herbert of its truth; he congratulated Wilkinſon on his happineſs, telling him his choice was the moſt lovely
creature he had ever feen; and added, with
his native franknefs, if fhe had been free,
he muſt have been her flave.

The neighbouring gentry, as thoſe in
that country are called, who live within
twenty miles, pouring in to viſit young
Herbert, occaſioned a fhort ceſſation to
the happy hours our two young friends
uſed to dedicate to the moſt refined friendfhip; Anna, at her earneſt requeſt, was
fuffered to ſtay at home till the buſtle was
over; and Miſs Herbert, when the com-

pany

pany confifted only of gentlemen, always joined her at breakfaft; fometimes her brother, whofe fraternal love would not fuffer his fifter to walk fo far alone, accompanied her; but as Anna felt a fomething like embarraffment in his company, which preventing her inviting him to ftay, he returned after the falutations of the morning. To the grief of Wilkinfon, however, they foon returned to their old mode; he, whenever he could break from his bufinefs, ftill attending on Anna.

Mr. Herbert was fond of mufic, he played on feveral inftruments, fang with tafte, and his voice was pleafing and melodious: Wilkinfon liked to hear Anna fing or play, but as to mufic, he could not diftinguifh a jig from Handel's beft compofitions, his fociety, which had been agreeable, became teazing and tirefome; his attention was rude, it robbed her of the converfation of a fenfible man, whofe pleafure, when he entertained her, fhone in his fine eyes; it was certainly ill bred in Wilkinfon to take his offered place, when he happened (which

indeed

indeed was oftner the cafe) to be fitting next her; and fhe could not conceive the reafon why, if they walked or rode out, he was at once eager to be near her, and yet refign his place the moment Wilkinfon came!

But it pleafed, fhe faw, Mr. and Mrs. Manfel; and Mrs. Herbert vifibly favoured his addrefs; therefore fhe faid nothing to them; and to him fhe had no opportunity, as he never touched on his paffion when alone, altho' he provokingly adopted in public the entire appearance of a favoured lover; this however, happened but twice a week; the intermediate fpace, no jealous lover to interrupt the morning rambles, or evening converfation, fhe was the object to whom Mr. Herbert addreffed both his fpeech and attention. Unconfcious of any wifh, but what was authorized by virtue and honour, and won by the modeft difplay of his own fuperior knowledge and learning, all referve wore off; fhe fang and played his favourite fongs, walked with him, and liftened, delighted, when he read, as he undertook to do, Milton,

Milton, which was his favourite author, to his mother and the two young ladies.

Thus happily paſſed Auguſt and September; but a letter which then arrived, announcing the intention of Miſs Edwin to honour them with a viſit, interrupted thoſe charming parties.

Two months before, Anna would have rejoiced to ſee Cecilia; now it would quite derange their amuſements; beſides, Miſs Edwin was in love with Mr. Herbert, and Mr. Herbert was in love with Miſs Edwin. Well, certainly love was no improver of converſation, as appeared in Mr. Wilkinſon, whoſe preſence interrupted it; and indeed ſhe ſo little liked ſuch ſociety, ſhe would ſtay at home; her work had been ſtrangely neglected; Mr. Herbert could not poſſibly now go on with Milton; Miſs Edwin would hardly attend to it; notwithſtanding he went ſo delightfully through thoſe beautiful paſſages.

Poſitively he ſhould not have his happineſs interrepted by her, while Miſs Edwin was with him.

Forming

Forming this plan, as she was crossing the vale, out of a winding path which opened to the road, appeared Charles Herbert; whether conscious she was out of humour by anticipation, from surprise, or from any other cause, she blushed deep as scarlet, and then instantly turned as pale as death.

Mr. Herbert, I have told my reader, was a good natured man, and compassion itself; he flew to her, and inquired, with undissembled anxiety, the reason of her agitated looks; apologised for his sudden intrusion, for which he acknowledged himself the more culpable, as the little copse of wood, out of which he came, hanging on the side of the hill, had concealed him from her sight, though he saw her from the time she had crossed the river, and he had come from it with a foolish intent to surprise her; but the fright he had put her in had been his severe punishment; he should not exist till she pardoned him.

Anna had by this time, recollected herself, and apologised in her turn for alarming him; but do you forgive me, Miss Mansel, said he, offering his hands;
will

will you be friends? Still holding them open to invite hers, which, after some hesitation, she extended to him. The glow of sensibility, added to the natural bloom of his complexion; he dropped with an involuntary emotion on one knee, as trembling he pressed it to his lips, exclaiming, as she much agitated withdrew her hand, forever hallowed be the sacred touch of spotless purity; how blessed the man on whom those eyes are turned with partial favour! Oh! Anna, still does the crimson glow animate that charming face, and still you are disturbed; fear not me, my lovely friend; be assured you are safe from every thought of injury. I would be the champion of yonr honour, my life's blood should freely flow in your defence, but my soul respects the union of hearts; not even for *you* would I tinge my honour with a wish to break the peace of confidential love; why then this silence, this reserve? Ah! exclaimed he, I see the reason!

Out of the opposite path from the wood, with hasty step and disturbed countenance, to the surprise of Anna, came Wilkinson,

A deeper

A deeper glow if poſſible now took poſſeſſion of her features, while he, without returning her ſalute, fiercely paſſed them; not knowing why, her confuſion increaſed, ſhe turned to look after him, and met the eyes of Herbert; bent on her with penſive, tho' obſervant looks. " I ſee, " Miſs Manſel," ſaid he, ſighing, " the " imprudence I have been guilty of; happy, " happy man; but I will ſet him right." With thoſe words he darted after him, leaving Anna without power to detain him; though ſhe wanted not inclination to rectify the error ſhe ſaw him under; he ſoon returned arm in arm with Wilkinſon, begging forgiveneſs for his behaviour.

Anna, bridling, ſaid, ſhe really was not offended; Wilkinſon attempted to take her hand; heavens, what an inſult! What would Charles Herbert think? Her eyes ſtruck fire.

I have before obſerved ſhe was very warm in her reſentments, and her countenance ſhewing the emotions of her mind, Mr. Herbert very prudently walked away, leaving the lover to plead his

own

own caufe; the moment he was gone, the
affured look it had coft' Wilkinfon great
pain to affume, dropped into dejeftion
and defpair.

Sadly convinced, no hopes now remained
for him, but thofe founded upon the miftake
of Mr. Herbert, he trembled at the idea of
a difcovery; yet he wanted not penetration
to fee that his conduft, far from concili-
ating the affeftion of Anna, provoked and
difgufted her; but ftill he had hopes, and
while thofe remained, could not prevail on
himfelf to change a conduft which appeared to be the only means of prefer-
ving it; but now, when alone with her,
who well knew the fallacy of the reports
he had circulated, or at leaft encouraged,
what could he plead in fupport of,
what plainly appeared to her, a piece of
contemptible art!

He fell at her feet, implored her compaffion; the artifice love had fuggefted
was the only one he knew, he had therefore only to give vent to his feelings to be
very eloquent; he deprecated her anger,
entreated her pardon, and pleaded the

A 5   irrefiftible

irresistible impulse of the fondest passion; he wept and kneeled alternately.

The heart of Anna, naturally soft and tremblingly alive to sympathy and compassion, was now unaccountably hardened; she saw, for the first time, a duplicity that hurt her the more, as it was plainly the effect of premeditated design; and when she reflected that Mr. Herbert, *(tho' his opinion was nothing to her)* was the dupe of that design, all the anger and resentment in her disposition was levelled at Wilkinson; and should she continue her walk to the castle with him, would it not be confirming by her own act, a deception on her friends. Quick as thought she turned from the possibility of again letting him triumph in his success, and without deigning to reply, went back to the village, and surprised her friends by her re-appearance at the parsonage.

CHAP.

CHAPTER XXVI.

A String of Resolutions.

WILKINSON followed her steps, tho'
all his pleading could not obtain an anfwer; she alledged a pain in her head as
the excuse for her speedy return, and immediately retired to her chamber, followed
by Mr. Manfel, who defired she would
have fome whey; she thankfully declined
taking any thing, faying a little reft
would certainly relieve her, and begged to
be left quite alone.

Her reflections on the tranfactions of
the morning were embittered by the difpofition of mind in which Charles Herbert
had left her; she again recalled to her memory every thing that had paffed; confufed
as she was herfelf, the trembling of his
hand as he held hers, yet dwelt on her

B 6 mind;

mind; his voice ever pleafing, was then modulated into a tendernefs that thrilled through her heart; with what feeling did he exprefs his friendfhip, amiable man! why fhould fhe deceive him? Why impofe on Mrs. Herbert and Patty; for great as their friendfhip, and unreferved as their intimacy had been, love had never been the fubject. of their confidence.

If Mifs Herbert had any attachment of that kind, fhe had not difclofed it to Anna; fhe had heard (who in the neigh-bourhood had not?) the terms Wilkinfon was on with her friend, and fhe obferved nothing in the behaviour of either, vio-lently to contradict it; but as Anna never entered upón the fubject, and as Patty rather avoided than fought her confidence, it was yet mentioned by them; the lover was evidently the moft fond and at-.tentive of men, and Anna the moft eafy and indifferent of women; but knowing her circumftances, it was na-tural to infer it was a match on her fide of conveniency, more efpecially as it

was not till very lately, (nor yet feen
by Mifs Herbert,) that Wilkinfon's civi-
lities were difgufting, or that he was very
rapidly incurring the diflike of her he loved.

Whatever were the young lady's reafons, fhe had been totally filent on the
fubject; but her filence appeared to Anna,
now that fhe revolved over every thing
that had paffed with refpect to Wilkinfon,
the effect of his artifices, and fhe refolved
no longer to fuffer her to entertain fuch
miftaken notions.

The deceiving her friend, was *ncw* a
matter of infinite importance; fhe would
beg Mrs. Manfel to decline the hateful
vifits of Wilkinfon; fhe would inform
Mrs. Herbert of her repugnance to the
match; fhe would intreat her dear Patty
to affift her in reconciling all parties to
her determination, of hearing no more
of a paffion fhe never had, nor ever could
approve.

This refolution cured the head ach;
and was no fooner formed, than, impatient
to put it in practice, fhe went down ftairs.

Mr.

Mr. Manfel was in his ftudy; the earneft and attentive pofture fhe found him in, liftening to Wilkinfon, who was in agitated and ferious difcourfe, together with the tears which were rolling down the wan cheeks of Mrs. Manfel, difconcerted and furprifed her; they were no lefs embarraffed at her appearance, which put a fudden period to their converfation.

But too much bent upon freeing herfelf from addreffes fhe fo much difliked, and determined on immediately throwing herfelf on the indulgence of Mrs. Manfel, her confufion for a moment only prevented the commencement of her plan; her head full of what it was her intention to fay to her friend, fhe begged her company round the garden; and full indeed it muft have been, to fuffer her to make fuch a requeft, as months had elapfed fince that lady had put her foot to the ground, her lamenefs obliging her to have a bed below, to which fhe was lifted, not being able to get up ftairs.

Mrs,

Mrs. Manfel looked her furprife, and without anfwering, pointed to her lame leg then on a ftool. Anna immediately felt the folly of her inconfiderate conduct, and ftill more difconcerted, begged her pardon, for having a moment forgot a Calamity, fhe fo fincerely deplored. To this apology, the tears of fenfibility and gratitude gave an unfpeakable grace, and all was forgotten.

Wilkinfon, to her great mortification, ftayed to dinner; a fervant foon after being fent by Mifs Herbert, to afk the reafon of Anna's not coming as fhe promifed, was returned with an excufe of her having been taken ill.

In the afternoon Mr. Manfel generally rode out, for the purpofes of giving his beloved wife the air behind him. Mrs. Manfel, as fhe had Anna at home, would have declined it; but *fhe*, ever forgetting her own in the intereft of her friends, urged them to go, not recollecting that fhe muft either ftay at home in the moft difagreeable *tête a tête* with Wilkinfon,

or

or by accompanying them, be feen again as his companion abroad; of two evils, fhe chofe the laft as leaft; a little pad they kept for her was therefore got ready, and out they fallied.

But as this was to be a day of mortification to our heroine, they had not gone a quarter of a mile from the parfonage, before they were met by Mr. and Mifs Herbert, coming to make a charitable vifit to their fick friend: The raillery of Mifs Herbert, not more than the grave looks of Charles, threw Anna into confufion; the very thing fhe had refolved to avoid, fhe was now doing. Wilkinfon kept his ftation clofe by her fide, and fpite of all fhe had refolved, again exhibited the fuccefsful lover. Patty, ignorant of what had happened, and ftill continuing good naturedly to rally, and chide her by turns, for difappointing them of the pleafure of her company, to the aftonifhment of all prefent, Anna burft into a violent flood of tears.

Mifs

Mifs Herbert, alarmed and grieved at the effect of her harmlefs mirth, made a thoufand apologies; Mr. Manfel's looks fpoke more than his words; and Mrs. Manfel's eye gliftened in fympathetic tendernefs; Wilkinfon was officioufly kind; Mr. Herbert's countenance underwent a thorough change; the grave caft gave place to tendernefs and compaffion, yet during their fhort ride he fpoke very little, and appeared glad when it was ended.

Mifs Herbert ftaid tea with her friend, but her brother fet off on a hard gallop before they entered the village, as his mother, he faid, would expect him; and Wilkinfon had half an hour's private converfation with the rector, before he waited on Mifs Herbert home.

The moment they were gone, Anna, whofe whole heart was full of her defign, and who had fuffered unfpeakably from the delay of a few hours, related the occurrence of the morning, and her indignation at Wilkinfon's conduct, which was increafed by the conviction, that he

wifhe d

wiſhed to make people believe ſhe was
engaged to him; and concluded with
begging that Mrs. Manſel would indulge
her, by declining his conſtant viſits, or
at leaſt permit her to refuſe his particular
attendance on herſelf.

Both her friends appeared much dif-
treſſed at the determined manner of her
expreſſing her diſlike, it grieved them to
find ſhe had taken to a perſon, whoſe dif-
intereſted affection they had hoped would
ſurmount all her objections. Mrs. Manſel anſwered, ſhe was exhauſted by her
ride, but would talk the matter over
with her in the morning; when, if ſhe
continued inflexible, they would preſs, what
in their opinion was of the greateſt moment
to her, no more.

Anna, who had always thought what her
governeſs ſaid,

Wiſeſt, virtuouſeſt, diſcreeteſt, beſt,

underſtood, to her great concern, that
what ſhe aſked, would, if granted, be
owing to their indulgence to her, in op-
poſition to their own judgment, as well
as wiſhes; and this idea doubled all her
obligations

obligations to them; they forebore to urge her to accept a fettlement, which would eafe them of the expence of fupporting her, an expence fhe trembled to think they could fo ill afford, as Mrs. Manfel's illnefs had been, and ftill was, of the nature to require the firft advice and affif-tance, which was procured with great coft, from the diftance at which doctors of any eminence refided.

It is true, Lady Edwin's generofity had been extremely acceptable to them on that account, but that was a refource not likely to continue; and to live always on the bounty of friends was infupport-able; yet to marry merely for a maintenance was worfe, as it was offering injury in return for love.

Thofe thoughts kept her awake moft part of the night, and fhe rofe in the morning to meet her friend, with pale face and fwelled eyes.

Mrs. Manfel flept very little better; her care for the welfare of the young perfon fhe tenderly loved, and for whofe profperity fhe had the moft maternal folicitude, in-

decreafe

-creafed, as her own feelings convinced her
fhe fhould be foon called from a world,
where, notwithftanding her chriftian refignation, her affections were fo ftrongly,
bound; fhe forefaw if Anna was not fettled, fhe muft have many difficulties to
encounter, and if Mr. Manfel fhould
likewife be called away, he had nothing
to leave her; alone, in a world, where innocence and honour are the common prey
of mankind, and where triumphant vice
looks into filence the pleas of modeft
merit, of what fervice would be the delicacy of her fentiments, the rectitude of
her principles, or the elegant fimplicity
of her manners? Her beautiful perfon, far
from being of advantage, what would it
excite, but the fpirit of feduction, in the
men, and envy in the women! Who would
protect her! and how would it be poffible
for her, whofe heart fought alliance with
all God's creatures, to be guarded againft
wiles, fhe had no conception of! or to fupport her difappointment, when, after mixing with mankind, fhe fhould be fadly
convinced, that the virtues fhe honoured,

and the benevolence she adored, exifted so sparingly among the sons of men.

Mr. Wilkinson had exceedingly alarmed and diftreffed her, by his account of the interview in the wood; he faw, or fancied he faw, a growing attachment between young Herbert and Anna; the firft he concealed, but gave the latter with all he had obferved, and all that fear and jealoufy painted to his own jaundiced imagination, in the moft glowing colour to Mr. and Mrs. Manfel; he exaggerated the youthful gaiety of Herbert into a fpirit of libertinifm, and adduced the diffipation of the father, the dependence of the fon on the Edwins, and the well known pride of that family, as reafons why it was impoffible, he could addrefs her on honourable terms.

Mrs. Manfel was too well acquainted with the innate purity of her pupil, to doubt her being betrayed into any blameable or imprudent act, but fhe was not fo fecure with refpect to her peace; fhe had a great fhare of fenfibility, and fo perfectly artlefs, that nothing like fufpicion approached

proached her ideas; ſhe was therefore the more likely to be the victim of credulity in her firſt impreſſions. Mrs Manſel's know-ledge of Herbert's family concerns con-firmed Wilkinſon's report, who, under ſo reſpectable a ſanction, ventured to hint the injury to the peace, as well as charac-ter, of Anna, her intimacy with ſo dan-gerous and inſinuating a young man, might produce; and added, the only effectual method to preſerve the honour of their relation, was to unite thier inte-reſt with his entreaties, to prevail on her to become his wife.

Mr. Manſel readily coincided with this advice; and the alarm given by the intel-ligence of the jealous lover being con-firmed by the behaviour of Anna, induced Mrs. Manſel to promiſe her influence, but at the ſame time ſhe conditioned with her huſband, that if they found the peace of Anna likely to be affected by her com-pliance with their requeſt, it ſhould be at once given up; and as the ſalt water had been preſcribed to Mrs. Manſel, ſhe would take her with them to Swanſea, where the

the rector had a relation, from whom
they had received ftrong invitations, and
keep her there till Mr. Herbert left
Llandore; abfolutely declining, though
much urged, to attempt to fetter her inclination.

When Anna attended her friend, overpowered with a fenfe of obligation, and
expecting the ftrongeft efforts in favour of
a man fhe thoroughly difliked, in the light
he propofed himfelf; forrow and apprehenfion deprived her the power of ut-
terance, and fhe ftood before Mrs. Manfel the emblem of filent dejection; the
tears rolled down her cheeks from her
averted eyes, but the kindnefs of her
maternal friend reaffured and comforted her; her queftions were equally
blended with kindnefs and wifdom; and
the cool, yet ftrenuous efforts made in
favour of Wilkinfon, had the aid of reafon and intereft to fupport them; his unbounded affection, his opulent·profpects,
prefent eligible fettlement, and unimpeached moral character, were urged in
oppofition to the repugnance avowed by

Anna,

Anna, who, aſhamed of having no argument to offer but what originated in ſe
while all thoſe of her friends were ſo noble, and uttęrly diſintereſted, heard in
ſilence the pleadings of friendſhip in be-
half of love, unable to procure from her a
ſingle hope, or to draw her out of a ſilence,
the moſt deciſive againſt the point ſhe had
ſought to carry. Mrs. Manſel, at length
aſſured her, that ſhe would no farther urge a
matter on which depended her peace in
an awful moment ſhe knew was approach-
ing; that her heart had built on it as the
ſweeteſt cordial, hope could give; that
when, in fond contemplation of the
beauties both of her mind and perſon, the
ſad proſpect of her deſtitute ſituation, when
ſhe ſhould 'be no more, (particularly if
Mr. Manſel was likewiſe to meet an early
fate) overcame her; that then ſhe ſought
and received conſolation in the ſecurity
of her peace and welfare, under the protection of an-honeſt man, whoſe principles and power were equally flattering to
her wiſhes: but if ſhe muſt give up this
darling proſpect, ſhe entreated Anna
would

would indulge her with one promife, which was that of confulting Mr. Manfel on the difpofal of her heart, before it was too late to recal it.

Anna, drowned in tears at this affecti-onate fpeech, delivered with a painful folemnity by the perfon fhe moft loved and refpected on earth, whofe countenance fpoke at once the ravage of ficknefs, and too, too plainly confirmed the melancholy prefage which flowed from her lips, in an agony of grief, threw herfelf at her feet.

Oh! my more than mother, cried fhe; her voice interrupted, and almoft choaked by the violence of her emotions, dear, bleffed monitrefs of my youth, ever kind and valued friend of my heart, fpare, oh! fpare your Anna; can I rob you of one moment's happinefs! is it *me*, who would die to give you pleafure, that takes from the peace of your dying hours; that fharpens the keen edge of pain? Oh! difpofe of me as you pleafe! I am yours! teach me how to repay the tendernefs you have fhewn my helplefs youth, to chear the heavy hour of ficknefs, and be affured

whatever

whatever are the secret sacrifices I make, however strong my repugnance, and unconquerable my dislike, I never never more will oppose your wishes, I will, bursting into fresh tears, if you bid me, to morrow give my hand to Mr. Wilkinson!

Oh! Anna, my dearest girl, returned Mrs. Mansel, this extorted consent must not be on so solmen an engagement; I doubted not but my entreaties would have this effect on your ductile heart; but to take advantage of your grateful sorrow for a departing friend, would be to engrave her on your memory, with the bitter accompanyment of remindless grief, without hope of change, but the awful one that will reunite us. I will urge you no more; be comforted, continued Mrs. Mansel; far be it from me to discourage my Anna, by insinuating, that the world, bad as it is, has no accommodation for innocence and virtue, without uniting them in opposition to inclination. But oh! my child, embracing her, though I could see you enter the busy scenes to which you are yet a stranger, without a single

appre-

apprehenfion for your honour, here even here, I tremble for your tranquility; be upon your guard; you are deferving of every thing; but alas! it is not the moft deferving that are the moft happy.

She then entreated the weeping orphan to preferve the fame appearance to Wilkinfon, till their return from the excurfion fhe propofed, when they would entirely put a period to addreffes which were fo difagreeable, but not once hinting her fufpicion of the partiality fhe had been accufed of; rightly concluding, if it had any other foundation than Wilkinfon's jealoufy, time, abfence, and her own good fenfe, would be much more likely to operate, while the fecret was confined to her own bofom, than if fhe had the leaft reafon to fuppofe it was difcovered.

CHAP.

CHAPTER XXVII.

Polite Friendſhip.

THE preparation they were now to make for their little journey, prevented ſo much of her time being ſpent at Llandore Caſtle; and another reaſon to reſtrain her viſits there, if ſhe were earneſt in her reſolutions, was the arrival of Cecilia Edwin, who with both her couſins, ſurprized Anna in a deep revere, looking acroſs the vale at the white chimnies of Llandore.

If the year which had paſſed ſince the meeting of Cecilia and my heroine, had matured the perſonal as well as mental graces of the latter, it had not been leſs buſy nor made fewer alterations, in thoſe of the former. The winter ſpent in London, where ſhe had been preſented, and

where

where her great fortune and family, and
their confequent attractions, had ftampt
their own value in pretty legible characters, on every part of her behaviour, and
actions, were circumftances that could not
fail of enlarging thofe ideas of gallantry,
which in her earlier years had influenced
her conduct, tho' they had not quite ef-
faced the impreffions love and heroifm
had made over her mind—She was at prefent a kind of middle character, between
a fentimental novelift, and a town coquette; her drefs was fo much to the very
extreme of the fafhion, that it was not in
the remote region of Llandore only fhe
was an object of wonder and curiofity, for
fhe had the fatisfaction of being gene--
rally ftared at in the metropolis.

Her clear brown complection, where the
blood had formerly been feen to mount on
every little occafion, was now hid by the
politer daubings of rouge; and her fine
gloffy black hair, loft in a pafte of pink-
powder and pomatum. Anna was the
fweeteft girl in the world, and her confi-

dential

dential friend, with whom she regularly corresponded; yet it was matter of wonder now how her cousin Patty could exist in that corner of the world, with no other companion than such a demure piece of still life; she was neverthelefs in raptures at the fight of her, though really it was with regret she obferved great alteration in her, and it mortified her to fay, thofe alterations were not for the better.

This opinion of Mifs Edwin, was not only contradictory to *our* fentiments, but her *own*; she felt that partial as she was to her *dear* felf, the advantage of her fweet friend, was too great for the candour, or fincerity of fo very fine a lady; but what ever other changes had happened in the courfe of the winter, Charles Herbert was still her male favourite, although it was no fault of Mifs Edwin, that she yet retained her name; a peer not much older than her father, Sir William, having been a very warm advocate for her changing it to his own, but was refufed by Lady Edwin,

win, on account of the obscure original
of his parent.

Cecilia Edwin finding in her collection
of new novels that the amiable heroines of
most of them were married, and not only
contrived to keep their old lovers, but at-
tract new ones, notwithstanding their co-
verture, found great temptations in the title
and riches of Lord Sutton, and not foreseeing
her mother's objection had already obliged
most of her corresponding friends with an
account of the severity of that fate, which,
in obedience to the commands of her parents, had obliged her to unite herself to
a rich disagreeable old man, while her
heart was attached to the most amiable,
the most charming youth in the world.

That youth she now shone on, in full
lustre, the regard he actually had for so
near a relation, the respect due to her rank,
and immense fortune, and the consideration
of family obligations, all operated on the
mind of young Herbert, and induced him
to treat Cecilia with affection as well as
politeness; when they walked, she hung

on

on his arm; he was her efcort when on horfe-
back; and tho' he faid he did not *now love*
dancing, when he was forced into it, Cecilia was his partner, and he was her beau
on every occafion; indeed, fhe had not a
doubt of her abfolute rule in his heart;
but however pleafing fuch a lover was in
the country, fhew, equipage, aud the dear
round of fafhionable pleafures, were in
London a thoufand times more delightful; fo that tho' fhe yet profeffed, and did
feel a penchant for her coufin Charles,
fhe by no means defigned him the fu-
preme favour of her hand and fortune.

Cecilia's idea of the increafing love of
Mr. Herbert was in fome degree confirmed
by an alteration in his temper, and fhe im-
puted it to the refpectful timidity that tied
his tongue; this alteration was, I muft
own, not of the moft brilliant kind; from
the beft tempered, chearful creature exift-
ing, he was become peevifh and melancholy; man delighted not him, whatever women might do; even Cecilia's company
was often avoided, and a folitary ramble
preferred

preferred to her lively converfation; his appetite failed, and a general languor pervaded his whole frame;. Mrs. Herbert, grieved at an alteration, which alarmed her for his health, and Mr. Herbert, who hated Wales himfelf, condemned that charming retirement as the caufe of his fon's change.

When the ladies furprifed our heroine, as I have related, at the parfonage, fhe was deep in thought on the inftability of all human felicity; Mifs Edwin's arrival at Llandore fhe had heard of, and figured to herfelf the fame happy parties, in which fhe had heretofore been; her feat in the grove, her voice in the Trio, her courted judgment and applaufe at the readings, were now affumed by Cecilia,—and a deep figh followed thofe reflections.—tears ftarting into her eyes, when they were dif- perfed by the fight of thofe who had ex- cited them.

Mifs Herbert feverely reproached our heroine for her long and frequent abfences from the caftle; and Cecilia infifted no-

C 5 thing

thing now muſt keep her from thence. The emaciated looks and weak ſtate of health in which they ſaw Mrs. Manſel, were Anna's beſt apology for the ſeeming neglect of her friends, and the intended journey to the ſea mentioned with regret, as ſhe would ſtill longer be deprived of the honour of attending them; the ladies, however, would not ſtir, without her pro- miſe of ſpending ſome part of every day with them till her departure.

Mrs. Manſel, tho' the company of my heroine was the only thing beſides that of her huſband's, in which ſhe delighted, conſidering the importance of the ac- quaintance of people of rank to her young orphan, readily conſented to their requeſt, and ſhe engaged to ſpend the next day with them.

This appointment was a dagger to the heart of Wilkinſon, who was preſent, but it was not to be prevented, nor, what was worſe, could he poſſibly attend her, as he was engaged to go to Briſtol on buſineſs of the iron works with Mr. Herbert; he

was

was loft in the anguifh of his own reflections when the Llandore family left the
parfonage, and as Anna, (intent on her own
thoughts, fat at the window, her eye eagerly following their fteps, as they de-
fcended the flope, but foon unable to
conquer her emotions) turned from the
fight of the gay Cecilia, hanging on the
arm of her coufin Charles, and meeting
the dejected look of her defponding lover,
all her diflike changed to pity.

Low fpirits, a complaint very new to
her, fhe had been lately much troubled
with; a fit now feized her, tears filled her
eyes, and fighs rent her bofom: Wilkinfon faw not one, nor heard the other; his
heart was too full of his own vexation, to
attend to any thing elfe; and to prevent a
renewal of the intimacy at the Caftle, was
the fubject of his prefent meditation; Anna
had long left the room before he was fenfible he was alone; no remedy, no invention
offering to aid his wifhes, he was obliged to
take leave of the family, with his heart torn
by regret, jealoufy and apprehenfion.

CHAP.

CHAPTER XXVIII.

More Love Matters.

THE next morning after having tried
every gown and cap her wardrobe afforded, and confulted for a much longer period than ufual, her glafs, before it was
poffible to determine on thofe moft becoming her complection, Anna at laft fixed on
a fprigged muflin gown, tied with lay-
lock ribband, a chip hat, decorated with
the fame colour, and her own fine hair,
faftened up with a comb.

Blooming and frefh as the blowing
myrtle in her bofom, fhe began her way
to the Caftle by the fame path, where fhe
had the interview with Herbert, which
was fo deeply engraved on her memory;
when the turning path prefented itfelf to
her view, her confcious blood mounted in

her

her cheek, a figh involuntary forced its way—fhe ftopped.

A ruftling among the trees announced an intruder, who appeared in the diftant figure of Herbert;—he was prefently before her.

He apologized for a fecond time intruding on her privacy, and afked with a fmile, " am I now in danger of interrupting an affignation ?"

Anna, picqued at the queftion, walked on with a flight courtefy.

The offence was increafed by a farther enquiry, whether the happieft of *all* happy men were to meet, or overtake her ?

When he fpoke intelligibly, fhe would anfwer.

He faw fhe was angry, he told her ; but froward fpirits, fpoiled by indulgence, were apt to be ungovernable.

" Meaning mine, Sir ? anfwered Anna. Oh, no ! returned he, fighing.

Mr. Wilkinfon's then ?

" Nor him neither !"

Your

. Your own Sir? fmiling.

Ah! anfwered Herbert, that fmile, that look!—yes, madam, I own, mine is the ungovernable, the froward, and repining fpirit, your indulgence has ruined.

Anna looked aftonifhed.

You are furprized—but do you conceive it nothing, to be bleft in your fociety! to hear the accents of divinity from your lips! to have no one defire beyond beholding you! to be fed by your fmiles, with the fond hopes of your friendfhip! and have thofe bleffings dearer, heaven knows, than exiftence, at once torn away! to fee abfence and cold referve take place of friendfhip, and condefcenfion ! Ah ! Anna, never, never may you feel the anguifh of unrequited *friendfhip!*

But I leave you—whatever are my own feelings, let me not a fecond time wound yours.

With thefe words, the unaccountable Herbert difappeared, leaving Anna in a ftate of mind, that would have again
tempted

tempted her return to the parsonage, had she not feared to alarm her friends.

With trembling steps she pursued the path to the Castle, and was met at a little distance from it by Miss Edwin and Patty Herbert; Charles soon joining them, in company with some young ladies and gentlemen, who by invitation dined there.

A harp and violin being in the neighbourhood, Mrs. Herbert procured their attendance; and a little ball in the afternoon gave Miss Edwin an opportunity of exhibiting to advantage her graceful person in a minuet with young Herbert; they were both deservedly applauded; and a young lady who sat by Anna, whispered her, the two cousins looked born for each other; it was pity they should ever be parted; did not she think so? She bowed assent, but her tongue refused its office. A partner in the country dances offering, she stood up, glad to escape a discourse, she found herself unable to support.

When

When they broke up and Mrs. Herbert's carriage waited to carry Anna home,.
her breaſt bow was loſt; ſhe was ſure ſhe
had it on when ſhe went down the dance;.
that Patty confirmed; ſome inviſible power
had certainly ſecreted it;—the room was
ſearched over and over; no bow could be
found, and ſhe was obliged to go home
without it; the ſame ill ſucceſs attended.
her enquiries next morning—it was no.
more heard of.

Anna continued her daily viſits to the
Caſtle; their party *quareé* was enlivened
by little concerts; Herbert played very
well on the flute; Cecilia took her harp,.
Patty her guittar, and Anna ſat to the
organ; they walked, they chatted; every
heart ſeemed in uniſon, even Cecilia's forgot its gay flirtations, and reſted on the
peaceful delights of friendſhip and retirement; but a ſad, a fatal reverſe awaited.
our young heroine.

Mrs. Manſel grew daily worſe; her declining health filled Anna with grief and.
anguiſh;

anguifh; the day was fixed for their departure, and fhe went for the laft time to
the Caftle, where as it was to be a farewel
vifit, fhe ftayed the night; the folemn
cloud which overfpreads the interview of
friends who are on the point of parting,
was never more vifible than in this evening
at Llandore Caftle; reftlefs and uneafy,
they all retired early; and the morning on
which Anna was to be taken from this
fcene of felicity, broke on her fleeplefs
eyes with little comfort, and lefs hope.

Tired of a bed on which fhe had unavail-
ingly courted reft, in hopes the air would
help to difpel the oppreffion of her heart,
fhe walked out; the dear fpot fhe was
about to leave contained her warmeft affections; Mifs Herbert would be gone, before fhe returned; Mrs. Manfel's health in
fuch a melancholy ftate, what alterations.
might not happen, for ever to divide her
from characters fhe loved and revered? Mr.
Herbert and Cecilia would undoubtedly
foon be united; God blefs them, faid fhe
aloud,

aloud, juſt as ſhe was met by the iden-
tical bridegroom her fancy had painted.

" And who, Miſs Manſel, is ſo happy as
" to be the object of your early oriſons ?
" had my friend Wilkinſon been here, he
" would have been pleaſed at your em-
" phatical *them*, ſince ſuch ſolicitude for
" one even of your own ſex, muſt be en-
" viable."

Is it not natural, Sir, returned ſhe, for
me, who have ſo many obligations to the
inhabitants of the place I am ſo ſoon to
leave, to be fervent in my wiſhes for their
happineſs ?

And were they then, Madam, the ſub-
jects of your thoughts ! and may I aſk,
were the males of the family included in
the bleſſing ?

Indeed, Sir, they were, ſaid Anna, with
the moſt engaging earneſtneſs and ſim-
plicity.

And God bleſs you too, moſt amiable
and lovely of women, anſwered Herbert;
" I have much to be forgiven for, Miſs
" Manſel;

" Manfel; but I know fo well the fweet-
" nefs of your difpofition, I have no fear,
" but my heart, if laid open at your feet,
" would be more the object of your com-
" paffion than refentment; if I have been
" the unhappy fource of uneafinefs to you,
" believe me it was without defign; the
" efforts of reafon, reflection, and ho-
" nour, may have been in fome few mo-
" ments fince I have known you, too
" weak to conquer feelings that have re-
" ceived additional ftrength from con-
" current circumftances, or to conceal
" wifhes incompatible with my own peace
" and yours; yet, in my lucid intervals,
" and thofe I truft are many, my whole
" foul is interefted in your honour and
" felicity; adieu, Madam, if my indifcre-
" tions revive in your imaginations, re-
" member in the moment when my heart
" was burfting with its fecret woe, . I
" prayed for your happinefs, and tore
" myfelf away."

" Remember!" repeated the agitated
Anna. " Oh! that I could learn to for-
" get,"*

" get," following his quick steps with her swimming eyes, as he left her.

It was not possible now to misconstrue his meaning; hopes, which he had hitherto repelled, filled her heart; his trembling, his faultering, his hesitation, could have but one source.

And am I then, said she, exultingly, beloved by Charles Herbert! who can tell, if blessed with birth and fortune, I might have been his choice; enviable attractions! did I ever regret your want before!

But I may admire his virtues, I may respect his principles, nay I may love the guarded purity of his passion, while I am single, without injuring myself or him; and what is there on this side heaven, that can give an equivalent for even so poor a gratification?

This interview gave Anna spirits; she returned to the house, and after spending the day there, she was fetched home by the rector, who then took leave of the young ladies, Mrs. Herbert having been so good as to take her tea at the parson-

age.

age with the worthy Mrs. Manfel, with whom fhe parted with the fincereft wifhes for the re-eftablifhment of her health, and regret for the occafion of their fepara- tion. Herbert did not appear; he had rode out, and returned not till Anna had left the Caftle.

CHAPTER XXIX.

The House of Mourning.

THE following morning Mr. and Mrs. Manſel, with Anna, ſet out for Swan-ſea.

Neither the ſalutary ſea breezes, nor the briny medicine, were of the leaſt ſervice to Mrs. Manſel, whoſe diſorder increaſed beyond all human aid; and her weakneſs ſometimes rendering it impoſſible to carry her in a chaiſe; willing to try every thing, ſhe was conveyed by water to the Briſtol Hot Wells.

Here ſhe continued till after Chriſtmas, in vain hopes of receiving benefit from the waters and phyſicians. Mr. Manſel's diſtreſs is not to be conceived.—To gratify him only, his beloved wife ſtaid there;

but

but at laſt, finding all would not do, ſhe begged to reſign her breath at the Parſonage; and ſo eager was the worthy woman to get there, ſhe ſupported herſelf in her long journey much better than could be expected.

She was brought in a litter the laſt four ſtages, followed by the tears and prayers of the inhabitants, through the village to her own houſe; where with an unruffled mind and quiet conſcience, ſhe waited the eternal fiat.

During the awful interval that paſſed between the time when every hope of her recovery had left them to that of her diſſolution, the anguiſh of her huſband and young friend may be better conceived than deſcribed.

The ſolemn and hopeleſs inquiries of the neighbours, the lamentations of the poor, the grief of the ſervants, were faint epitomies of the ſevere ſorrows of the inconſolable huſband, and of the affection-tae orphan.

The

The parfonage, fo late the fcene of perfect tranquility, of chearful content, and
uninterrupted peace, was now literally a
houfe of mourning.

In this fcene of poignant forrow, although every moment when abfent from
the dying faint's apartment, Anna was
drowned in tears by her bed-fide fhe was
the ferene companion of the friend fhe loved; fhe was her nurfe, fhe read to her; and
when the broken-hearted hufband could
officiate in his holy office, fervently joined
in the facred devotion of a death bed;
while Mrs. Manfel dofed, with true filial
piety fhe exerted her utmoft power to comfort the grieving rector, though her own
feelings were unfupportable.

On the 28th of January, after very ftrong
ftruggles for one who had been gradually
weakening fo long, it pleafed God to take
to himfel a woman who had ferved him
all her days: her refignation and fortitude
during her painful and lingering diforder,
was the laft, and not leaft valuable leffon
left to Anna, in whofe arms fhe expired;
and

and who, contrary to the modes of the times which authorifes depofiting the corpfe of our beft friend in a vacant apartment, continued to fit and fleep in the room until the eighth day; when, having (led by Mr. Manfel, and followed by the parifhioners of Llandore) feen her remains depofited in the chancel of the church, they retired, each to their apartments, unable to meet at that table where now the voice that cheered and inftructed, was heard no more.

Her laft injunctions to Anna were to follow the counfel of Mr. Manfel; and her laft requeft to her hufband, never to forfake or deny parental care to the child of her heart.

Mr. Manfel had a miaden fifter who had been fent for by Mrs. Manfel (when at Swanfea fhe faw no hope of her fpeedy return) to take care of the family, and had, at Anna's requeft, been continued in the houfe. After Mrs. Manfel's death, her ftay was ftill neceffary; but if it had not been fo, fhe would have had no inclination to leave a warm, full houfe, for her own little cottage, where she lived on a very small income.

Mrs. Jane Mansel was in the fiftieth year of her celibacy, and valued herself on her notability and fine shape; few women could vie with her in either; she was, indeed, saving to a proverb, and small to a fault: she was ill tempered, sandy haired, and sallow complectioned; she had not yet given up the hopes of matrimony, for which purpose, ever since she had resided at the Parsonage, she had been making a hoard of every thing in kind to tempt, where no other attraction was to be found.

Such a substitute for the saint they had lost, soon occasioned an alteration in the parson's family: the man and maid, who were the happy domestics of the best manager and mistress on earth, resigned their places, which were immediately filled by those, who knew nothing more than was necessary in a common farm house, and who, from a similarity of minds and manners, were the favourites of Mrs. Jane.

When

When Mr Manfel was prefent, nothing could exceed the fawning fpecioufnefs of this woman's behaviour to Anna; but the moment his back was turned, her never-failing topics were leffons of induftry to young people, delivered *to* her maid, but evidently meant *at* Anna.—She hated to fee thofe who are able, and having no-thing of their own, unwilling to work, loitering about as if their whole bufinefs in the world was to be maintained at other people's expence.

Thofe lectures, which had always wit-neffes, and her own want of fpirits, which were funk to the loweft ebb, foon leffened the confequence of Anna at the Parfon-age, and placed her in a fituation very little to be envied. She did not like, by inform-ing Mr. Manfel of his fifter's conduct, to embroil him in family difpute, and much lefs did fhe choofe to fubmit to the infults of a woman; who, if fhe had been of a to-lerable temper, was fo extremely ignorant and low bred, it was impoffible to affo-ciate with her.

Mr. Manfel's grief for his wife was of
the kind to laft long; it vented not itfelf
in words, it fubfided not in the overflowings which dropped from his *eyes*; his foul
was the manfion of integrity; *there*, in
every fentiment, in every thought, he
found renewed the memory of his Maria:
nothing of goodnefs ftruck his imagination unaccompanied with her idea; the
violence of his forrow, indeed, abated, as
he brought himfelf to confider fhe had
but preceded him in the rich reward of
virtue. But when alone, when he could
uninterruptedly recal her voice, her action,
and her wifdom, he fancied himfelf yet
in her fociety; he was, therefore, feldom
vifible but in the difcharge of his duties
and at meals; nor was it always that he
accompanied them on thofe occafions;
the chearful board, the innocent chat, the
comfortable firefide were now no more; and
Anna fo conftantly reminded of this, began to conceive the living a burden on
honeft pains-taking people, fhameful and
unneceffary: yet loath to hurt or offend

Mr.

Mr. Manfel, it was with great reluctance, and not till perfonally and directly affronted by Mrs. Jane, fhe could raife her fpirits fufficiently to propofe leaving him.

Mr. Manfel heard her with forrow and furprife; he entreated her to confider well the ftep fhe was taking; queftioned her about his family; begged fhe would modulate it as fhe pleafed. Wilkinfon, though he called fometimes, had received his definitive anfwer: *he* was no longer troublefome, what could be her motives?

Fully refolved to conceal the cause of her difguft, and too much irritated to remain fubject to the ignorant caprice of Mrs. Jane, fhe faid it was neceffary for her to lay down fome plan for her way of life. Servitude muft be her laft refource: fhe heard there were means in the metropolis by which women of good education might earn a decent fubfiftence, with a tolerable appearance: and another ftrong motive for her wifhing to go, was her defire to learn every particular of her origin, that

fhe

she might try to get some knowledge of her family.

Mr. Mansel, who knew it was not in his power to provide longer for her than he lived, felt the propriety of her reasons though he secretly wished she had not been so nice about servitude, as he thought the Edwins might have assisted her: he, therefore, ceased to oppose her intentions, but took every method to make her journey comfortable.

The fifty pounds Lady Edwin sent her remained untouched, notwithstanding all the money Mrs. Mansel had saved was expended, and some debts unavoidably contracted; this money and Mrs. Mansel's clothes he insisted on her taking; every thing belonging to her departed friend was dear to her: but as to the note, all his pleadings could not induce her to take more than twenty pounds.

Still the good man was very loath to part with her; but finding her bent on going, he took her himself to Brecknock, and having obtained the promise from her of

returning

returning to him, as her home, they parted with tears and regret on both fides; his laft words as he put her in the coach being, "Remember you have a horne, and " I am your father."

CHAPTER XXX.

A Journey to London.

ANNA took Bath in her way, and was received by Mrs. Herbert and Patty with the fame kindnefs and friendfhip fhe was ufed to at Llandore. They preffed her to ftay but fhe was too eager to get to London, to comply with their invitation. She hinted to them her circumftances, and Mrs. Herbert infifted on troubling her with a card to Lady Edwin, Cecilia being with Mifs Turbville in Bedfordfhire;

and Patty told her, with great joy, that her Coufin Hugh, who was expected every day, was to be married as foon as he came, when they fhould all be in London. They agreed to continue their correfpondence; and after two days ftay, Anna again fet out on her journey.

She was met by Mr. Dalton at the inn, who was apprized of her coming by a letter from Mr. Manfel.

The time which had paffed fo happily with our heroine, had produced many alterations in the fituation of Dalton; the clergyman, to whofe humanity he owed his curacy, was dead, and his fucceffor chofe to place a relation of his own in the cure. A twelvemonth had paffed without any profpect of again meeting an employ that would feed his family. Unfuccefsful in all his applications for a church, he, at laft, fought favour among his old friends the Methodifts; from one of thofe people he got a recommendation to a gentleman who headed and patronized the fect, and was indeed a good Samaritan.

In

In poſeſſion of a large and clear eſtate, as well as merchandize to all parts of the globe, Mr. Thornhill had the power of putting into practice the lovely attributes of charity and benevolence, as literally laid down by his divine Preceptor; to feed the hungry, to clothe the naked, and to pour balm into the wounds of enemies as well as friends, were the buſineſs of his life; if, in the extenſive line of his charities, he knew a preference, it was to the ſtrict profeſſors of his own religion; a partiality the more excuſable, as never the afflicted of either ſex were turned unrelieved from his gates. This gentleman, in the fervency of his zeal, had lately built a ſmall chapel in a village about ſix miles from the metropolis; the number of artificers employed in its neighbourhood was a temptation to the good man to endow it, and place there a preacher who would be attentive and induſtrious in his holy calling.

Dalton's application for charity, as a preacher with a numerous offspring out of

D 5 bread,

bread, and deftitute of means for rheir fupport, fortunately came at this period to the
hands of Mr. Thornhill, whofe compaffion for the individual was increafed by his
general good will to his fellow creatures,
on whofe account the chapel was erected;
he relieved the neceffities, painted in a very
ftrong light by Dalton, and placed him
in the new meeting, rent free, and gave
him fifty pounds a year for life. In this
fituation he was when he received the unwelcome news of Anna's return to his protection; however, by his wife's advice, he
went to the inn where the coach ftopt, in
order to conduct her to his houfe.

Mrs. Dalton received her very kindly,
and her kindnefs was much encreafed by
the prefent of a brown fatin night gown of
Mrs. Manfel's for herfelf, and all the remains of the finery brought from Melmoth
Lodge, as well as the clothes fhe had out
grown fince, for her children, who were
difpofed of different ways, exeept the eldeft
daughter, who had ferved out her appren-
ticefhip to the mantuamaker, and now
worked

worked at her bufinefs, paying her father for her board and lodging.

The next morning Dalton told Anna, with very little ceremony, it was time for her to think of fome mode of living, without being a hanger-on from one to the other. Thefe were her own fentiments; but fhe could have difpenfed with his coarfe opinion on the matter, delivered without feeling or judgment. The contraft between this addrefs and thofe fhe had lately been ufed to, ftruck her fo forcibly, fhe could not immediately anfwer; and her filence being interpreted by him into a defign of fixing herfelf on him, he wifely refolved to let her know, fhe muft not expect to live with him; and he was on the point of being ftill lefs attentive to the laws of hofpitality, when a queftion from her brought the blood into the cheeks of himfelf and his wife.' It was to know the particulars of his firft meeting her; when and where it was; and laftly, what the things that were brought by the de-.

ceafed to the lodgings confifted of, and what was become of them?

After a little paufe, which, if our heroine had the leaft knowledge of guilt herfelf, muft have given birth to fufpicions not very favourable to her reverend friend, he told her where fhe was brought by her father, but that not only the woman who came with her was moved, that the very houfe (which was true) was pulled down, and another built on the fpot; that the things confifted of a few wearables, which had been fold without referve to defray the expences of the funeral; and that he had, by advertifement, and every enquiry in his power, endeavoured to find out to whom fhe belonged, without fuccefs; that by the fun-burnt complexion of both the man and woman, he concluded they came from abroad.

This account entirely banifhed every hope of learning any thing of her origin. It was very unlikely fhe, who was fo entirely ignorant of the world, fhould fucceed better in her refearches than Mr. Dalton,

ton, who was fo much interefted in finding fome one to take off his hands, a child,
who had no other claims on him but thofe
of charity.

Her next thought was to deliver Mrs.
Herbert's card to Lady Edwin, in hopes,
by that Lady's patronage, fhe might be
able to fix on fome means for her future
fubfiftence.

She accordingly went in the morning
ftage, and was fet down in Whitechapel.
The ftreets were very dirty; wholly unacquainted with London and its cuftoms,
fhe had no idea of taking a coach; through
the wet, therefore, fhe walked, inquiring
at every turning the way to Grofvenor-
fquare, which fhe reached in three hours,
having fometimes received right directions, and oftener wrong, to the great
entertainment of the witty crackers of fo
pleafant a joke.

Tired and fplafhed, at length fhe arrived at the door of Lady Edwin, which two
or three chairs and a dozen powdered fops,

in

in livery furrounded: thefe fhe had to push her way through.

The impudence, the vices, and the follies of their employers, are, in general, fo exactly copied by thofe party-coloured gentlemen, that when I have faid thofe in waiting belonged to fome of the firft and moft diffipated families in the kingdom, I need not add, the fight of a modeft young woman had in it too much novelty to pafs unnoticed or infulted. With great difficulty (as they ran all their undaunted faces under her hat) fhe reached the porter, who, with a fettled grin and witty fneer at his companions, ftood waiting to receive her.

To her modeft queftion of, " Is Lady " Edwin at home ?" fhe was anfwered with a gruff, No, and a fupercilious ftare; and then unfortunately her fpotted clothes, attracting the notice of the too-well-kept, idle wretches round her, fhe was faluted with a loud laugh.

Aftonifhed at fuch brutal rudenefs, fuch wanton unprovoked infolence, and terrified with the apprehenfions of what infults might

might farther be offered her, she was haftily going from the door, when a footman belonging to the houfe, ftruck with her beauty, recollecting Lady Edwin's woman had juft difcharged her maid, and promifing himfelf (for he was a perfon of great gallantry) his prefent condefcenfion might be rewarded with future favour, bid her come in, and civilly afked her bufinefs. Mrs. Herbert's name electrified the whole crew; thofe belonging to the vifitors' chairs flunk off, and the furly porter taking the card, rang for Lady Edwin's own man who begged her to walk in; at the fame time opening the door of an elegant and fpacious parlour, faid his lady had company, but he would deliver the card the moment they went.—Here to her great comfort she found a large fire, at which she dried her feet, and had time to fet her clothes in a little better order, as it was full two hours b efore she as admitted to Lady Edwin.

The cordiality of her reception made ample amends for the mortifications she
had

had received at the door: the lady em-
braced her with great affection, condoled
with her on her fable drefs, and expreffed
herfelf much pleafed at Mrs. Herbert's
fending her to Grofvenor-fquare.

Struck with a kindnefs fhe did not expect, our heroine burft into tears.

Lady Edwin's goodnefs increafed with
this mark of fenfibility; fhe had a real regard for her, and when fhe heard from
Mrs. Herbert, the declining ftate of Mrs.
Manfel's health, fhe thought the having
fuch a young perfon about her in quality of
a companion, would be both convenient
and agreeable:—Mifs Edwin troubled her
with very little of her company; fhe grew
corpulent and indolent; public places fhe
was weary of, and going out much fatigued
without amufing her. Lady Edwin liked
cards, and her routs were crowded by the
firft people; but there were many hours
which an elegant fenfible young woman
would very acceptably fill; fhe, therefore,
directly propofed to Anna living with her
on the footing of a companion, and faid
fhe

ſhe would compliment her with fifty pounds a year for clothes.

It cannot be doubted but this offer was gratefully accepted; and ſo deſirous was the lady of having her immediately there, an early dinner was ordered, and the coach carried her to Dalton's, with directions to wait for and bring her back.

When Dalton ſaw ſo elegant a carriage ſtop at his door and Anna alight from it, he could ſcarce believe his eyes; withundiſſembled joy he heard how fortunate ſhe had been; he congratulated her upon her more brilliant proſpects and, never out of his way, begged, if an opportunity offered, ſhe would put in a word for him to Lady Edwin, whoſe poor countryman he was.

Her baggage not having been unpacked was ſoon ready, and once more Mr. Dalton had the pleaſure of ſeeing himſelf freed from his care of Anna : ſhe returned to Groſvenor-ſquare early in the evening :— Lady Edwin, very much pleaſed with the gratitude and alacrity ſhe had ſhewn, ordered a piece of black ſilk in addition to what she already had, and gave directions to her own tradespeople to equip her in a fashionable stile, as her night was to be the third after.

In the intermediate space she did not fail acquainting Mr. Mansel with her situation, or thanking Mrs. Herbert for the friendly recommendation which had procured her the honour of Lady Edwin's favour, a hair-dresser having cut and tortured her charming ringlets into likeness of nothing human, and dressed in fashionable mourning, Anna followed Lady Edwin into her drawing room.

CHAP.

CHAPTER XXXI.

High Life.

LADY Edwin's doors opened at nine, but it was near eleven before the card tables were all filled. This fcene was perfectly novel to our heroine, and excited no lefs curiofity than wonder; fhe, who had hitherto looked on vifiting as a method of keeping up the connection of families and friends, could not conceive the pleafure of entertaining fuch a number of people by a fingle courtefy to each perfon as they entered, and an arrangement of the tables, any·more than fhe could reconcile it to her ideas of civility for people to leave the houfe without even that little ceremony, or beftowing a look at the lady of the manfion; the conftant fucceffion of feathered ladies and painted beaus. who juft glided round the

the rooms and retired, particularly ftruck
her, as a very unmeaning mode of paff-
ing their time.

She was, however, drawn out of one
furprife and thrown into another, by a moft
polite and flattering addrefs from a male
figure, who begged Lady Edwin to introduce him to the lovely ftranger; her lady-
fhip's ready compliance with this requeft,
convinced Anna it was a perfon of confequence who made it, which his ridiculous
appearance rendered at firft rather doubt-
ful, to one who knew not that nothing in
that ftile was beneath our modern nobles.

He was a tall, elderly perfonage, whofe
fatin waiftcoat and breeches were out-
pinked by the rouge on his cheeks, and
that beautifully contrafted by the white
daubings on the other parts of his hag-
gard face; he had a wide mouth, which
the art of his dentift contrived to fill
with a double row of falfe teeth; he was
fond of his height, and to keep up the
appearance of youth and vigour he wore
ftays; he was of fuch a amorous conftitution, that the fight of beauty to him

in a flame, and the fhew and variety of
his miftreffes could only be equalled by
his ftud of horfes; his hair was curioufly
frized out at the fides, in clofe imitation of
the royal Adonis; he wore a blue ribband
and was vaftly addicted to falling in love.

He approached Anna with a ghaftly
ftare, which he miftook for a languifhing
ogle, and which would certainly have provoked her rifible faculties, had not Lady
Edwin announced him the Duke of ——.
To laugh at a Duke would have been
fhocking; to refpect him impoffible; fhe
was, therefore, an angel, a goddefs, and
every thing divine, without raifing her vanity; and his Grace wounded, miferable,
and dying, without exciting her pity; fhe
had too much good fenfe to feel any thing
but contempt, for a man, whofe ambition
it was to take the lead in folly and diffipation, when not only his age but conftitution called for reformation and warm
flannels, and was not long able to conceal
her difguft; the ducal title filled her with
awe, but the poor animal who bore it
foon

foon deprived himfelf of refpect; fhe involuntary turned her back on his eloquence, his dignity, and his admiration.

The marked manner in which his Grace fingled out our heroine, called forth the glances of the beaus, who, dear creatures! to a man are all purblind; and the ladies, not to be behind them in defects, were fo good as to lifp out their inquiries of " Who is fhe, and what is fhe?"

Thefe general obfervations made her truly ridiculous; fhe actually was out of countenance; her modeft eyes withdrew from the gaze of curiofity; a piece of ill-breeding any modern belle would try to blufh at. But poor awkward thing fhe foon ceafed to be an interefting object, except to a few diffipated married men; for it being by fome means whifpered, that fhe was the daughter of a Welfh parfon, whom Lady Edwin had taken as a companion to Mifs Edwin, the ladies were eafy and the beaus fatisfied.

This, far from mortifying Anna, left her to enjoy her own obfervation, which brought

home

home things to her recollection lefs defirable than poverty and dependence. The infipid evening paffed, and the rooms cleared at one o'clock; Sir William, Lady Edwin, and Anna, then fat down to fupper, and retired about two.

One evening Mifs Manfel received a leffon for all the company they received, or the vifits they paid; and very foon was fhe fo well acquainted with the etiquette on thefe occafions, as to take all fatigue from Lady Edwin, who fat down to cards in the firft party, leaving the ceremonial part to her. When fhe was entirely fettled, and her thoughts at liberty, nothing to wifh for but the continuance of Lady Edwin's favour —the paft fcenes would often return to her imagination, was it poffible, was fhe indeed fettled under the roof of Lady Edwin, could it be, and fhould fhe again fee and converfe with Charles Herbert? Yes, fhe remembered his parting words; but, alas! what end could it anfwer? Better, far better would it be to forget he exifted; was he not engaged, and that

to

to her friend, the daughter of her benefactrefs; was it not unjuft and ungrateful to
wifh to fupplant a perfon, who had fo
many claims to a contrary conduct? And,
indeed, if that were not the cafe, if he
were free, were it likely he would think of
her, would his family pride ftoop to a girl
in her dependent ftate, one who had not the
benefits common to the refufe of fociety,
who knew not a creature of her blood,
and who was totally deftitute of the
means of fubfiftence but from the charity
of ftrangers? Certainly no; well, then,
fhe would refolve to think no more of
him :—but

   " Thought repelled, refenting, rallies,
   " And doubles every woe."

A letter from Mr. Manfel, in which the
good man favoured her with advice and
congratulations on her prefent fituation,
contributed not a little to the fixing in her
mind an idea that, to fay the truth, never
left it. He warned her againft the decep-
tions of her own heart, hinted at the partiality fhe was fufpected of having for

young

young Herbert; at the fame time he reprefented the impoffibility of its being attended with fuccefs; faid the dependent fituation of that young gentleman was fuch, that his ruin muft be the confequence of a fufpicion of that kind in the family, as he knew it was their fettled intention to unite him to his coufin; he begged, therefore, fhe would guard her peace (her honour he knew to be fecured by her own principles) he prefented Wilkinfon's beft wifhes and invited her home whenever fhe pleafed.

Anna fhed tears over this letter, and called herfelf feverely to tafk for her conduct, fome part or other of which muft have given rife to her friend's conjecture; and, perhaps, to others?—— Alarmed at this conclufion, fhe refolved to be more guarded in future.

Lady Edwin grew more pleafed with her companion the longer fhe knew her; and Sir William was as partial as generous, continually buying fome little trinket to prefent her with, and her time paffed, if not happily, at leaft agreeably.

CHAP.

CHAPTER XXXII.

The Arrival of a Stranger.

A Month after Anna's removing to Grofvenor-fquare, Mr. Hugh Edwin returned from abroad.

This event filled the houfe with joy; he was the idol of his family, and the heir of their noble fortunes; had been four years making the grand tour; no expençe or pains had been fpared to render him the moft accomplifhed man of the age, and his fine natural parts gave flattering hopes of the figure his rank and fortune entitled him to cut in the world.

But the high opinion entertained of his abilities by his fond parents, and their blind indulgence to the foibles of his infancy,

had

had ruined the one, and converted the other into mature vice.

He was handsome and elegant in his person; and by his acquaintance with the world, had acquired an easy and polite address.

His good understanding was embellished with a pleasing delivery, and when he chose to exert himself, he was. master of great elocution, which, added to a perfect knowledge of the laws of his country, promised to his father, who doted on him, the utmost that fame and ambition could bestow.

But the unrestrained liberty of action, and power of purse, which he received from the affection of his parents, involved him in almost every vice in the composition of human nature, and young as he was in years, returned to his country a veteran in iniquity—He had seduced under a solemn promise of marriage, before he went on his travels, a young widow of fortune and family, whose love for him so far exceeded all other considerations, that

though

though fhe found herfelf ruined and deceived, fhe accompanied him abroad,
when notwithftanding his great allow-
ance from his father, he contrived to
fpend her whole fortune.

She had bred by him, but as it is faid,
there is no friendfhip among the wicked,
neither can there be a lafting efteem or
real happinefs in a vicious connection.

The lover was inconftant, the lady jealous, and at the time of their return to
England, they, who had flattered themfelves
with the expectation of being bleffed for life,
were become mutual plagues to each other:
the unhappy woman, indeed, ftill doted on
her feducer; but paffion, founded on mere
fenfual pleafure, is fure to evaporate in difuft.

Edwin, certain of his father's generofity, made him immediately acquainted
with his fituation: he was not miftaken;
Sir William Edwin had the moft guilelefs
of human hearts; when the young pro-
digal protefted his forrow for his paft in-
difcretions and promifed, amendment,
the fond father believed him, and took

on

on himfelf the care of providing for the lady, which he generoufly did, and that in a manner that rendered her acceptance of five hundred a year, rather a favour conferred on, than received from him.

CHAPTER XXXIII.

Filial Piety in fafhionable Life.

EDWIN, now free from his companion, was at large; intrigue was his hobby horfe, and mifchief his pleafure.

The lovely Anna, in full bloom of beauty and innocence, was an object too defirable to be paffed over; his mother's

pro-

protection had nothing in it facred enough to preferve her from his attempts, nor his promife to his father confidered from the moment he had obtained his end; he knew Mifs Turbville was the deftined partner of his hand, but that, he never defigned, fhould fhackle his inclinations; the more he faw of Anna, the more he was enamoured witn her; and fo rapidly was her influence increafing, that it was with difficulty he could conceal his rap- tures, even in the prefence of his father and mother—Whenever he caught her alone, which he watched eagerly for, he pleaded his paffion with all the violence natural to his temper.

How eafy is it to refift temptation our inclinations revolt at! Anna could paint to Edwin his undutiful behaviour to the beft of parents; fhe could affure him, if there were no other objection, her obligations to Lady Cecilia would fufficiently fteal her heart againft addreffes fhe knew they would difapprove—Abandoned as this young man was, Anna's propriety of conduct and modeft dignity of deportment, were

fuch,

such that, he had hinted at nothing short of an honourable passion, although he was sensible it was neither in his power or inclination to perform an honourable engagement, if he could prevail on her to accept it.

But of that there was not the least danger; for though no more of his character had reached the ears of Anna than what Lady Edwin thought proper to disclose, she was armed with the argument I have hinted at; and had there been no other, I am persuaded there needed none; but in truth there was, and had young Edwin offered her a diadem, her heart was so devoted to the humbler graces of his cousin, she would have rejected him——

She lived but for Herbert, at the same time that she had not the most distant hope of ever being happy in the object of her choice; on the contrary, while her imagination was perpetually bringing back the last scene at Llandore, she flattered herself she could see him united to Miss Edwin, without any other emotion than what the most disinterested friend-

ship

ship would warrant, referving only to herfelf the pleafing idea, that while fhe was
fingle, (which fhe pre-determined fhould
be as long as fhe lived) fhe might conti -
nue the fecret preference which her heart
now gave him, without injury either to
his honour or her own; and having made
up her mind in this dangerous manner,
fhe no longer fought to reprefs the approbation, which in fpite of herfelf, would
accompany the memory of every action.

Her heart was continually forming
comparifons between him and the young
men that vifited at Sir William's; if her
fentiments happened to be thofe of - any
other perfon, fhe was fure Charles Herbert's expreffions would have given grace
to them; if fhe was difgufted, her firft
thoughts were, good heavens, how different is Herbert!

Thus, nourifhing the fecret bias of
her foul, fhe lived at Lady Edwin's
without any difquiet, but what the young
man's affiduities gave her, fome weeks:
for Mifs Edwin was to ftay in Bedfordfhire till the family went to fetch her,

that

that a convenient opportunity for Mr. Edwin's falling in love with Miss Turbville might not be wanting.

Mr. Edwin found himself in no hurry to forward this marriage; his heart became really devoted to Anna, the more seriously, that notwithstanding the disadvantages of her situation, two gentlemen of fortune, one of them of rank, had made their offers of marriage; one a Baronet, of good estate and reputable family, turned of forty; the other, a Mr. Mordant, a young man of unexceptionable morals, and agreeable person, son to an opulent West-India planter, who Sir William, being acquainted (with his connections) was very kind to; and he was admitted into the family on the footing of a relation; his father left him to his own choice of a wife, that must accompany him to Jamaica, and his heart paid homage to the charms of our heroine.

The indifference with which she received those proposals, and the explicit

man-

manner in which fhe refufed them, appeared no lefs extraordinary to Sir William and his lady, than flattering to the
vanity of their fon: he had been fo ufed
to fuccefs among the women, he could
not doubt but his good fortune would ftill
continue; and the latent partiality for his
dear felf, convinced him thofe rejections
of Anna were founded on her attachment
to him.

He dreaded nipping in the bud the
bright hope on which fo much depended;
the leaft hint of his nuptials, as confented to by himfelf, would, he forefaw,
ruin him with her. On Sir William fet-
tling his affairs with Mrs. Mitford, he
promifed to comply with all his wifhes in
regard to his eftablifhment in life: and
indeed a fituation, independent of con-
trol, was too defirable a matter to be declined by a young man who wifhed for nothing more.

Yet the lovely Anna to be given up, was
too great a facrifice even for independence,
and one excufe followed another to protract
time,

time. Mr. Herbert's family were invited to accompany them to Bedfordſhire, but Edwin had privately written to Charles to put off the journey from week to week, till Sir William declaring he would go without them, (their abſence would no longer anſwer his purpoſe) the day before their arrival, he thought proper to fall ſick, a private emetic gave the appearance of a violent attack that alarmed his parents, who wiſhed to call in every medical aſſiſtance; but their ſon had a particular confidence in one only, and he, though not a perſon who attended the family, was employed, and his reports of the progreſs of the diſorder juſt ſuch as ſuited the patient's inclination.

It was in vain Lady Cecilia intreated he would have more advice; it teazed him to be oppoſed, and increaſed his fever; he was ſure he was perfectly ſafe in the hands of Mr. Depuis, and would ſee nobody elſe.

Anna, ſuſceptible to all the feelings of humanity, and who loved and honoured

Lady

Lady Edwin, caught from her the habit
of folicitude for her fon; and anxious to
calm the fears of the fond mother, was
conftantly inquiring after the health of
her heir.

Of this circumftance Mr. Edwin's valet took care to inform his mafter, whofe
joy, at each proof of her attention was
hardly to be kept within bounds; to
her inquiries he was always better; to
others worfe: fo that Lady Cecilia, finding herfelf comforted by Anna's report,
was fo exceedingly pleafed when fhe made
it, that fhe could not but be encouraged
to perfevere in a conduct fo acceptable
to her patronefs.

In this fituation the Herberts found
them. Young Edwin and Charles had
fpent their youth, and taken the firft ru-
diments of learning together, having never been feparated till Mr. Edwin went
on his tour; fo that, unlike as the cou-
fins were in their principles, they were
much attached to each other.

Herbert

Herbert was hardly seated by the bed of his friend (for he pretended he could not sit up) before he disclosed his sham sickness, alledging his repugnance to the state of marriage at all times, but more particularly now, when he said he was expected to fall in love with one woman while he was heart and soul devoted to another, as the reason of putting this deception on his family; he then proceeded to inform him of the method he had taken, having actually made himself ill by counterfeiting sickness.

This occasioned a good deal of mirth between the two friends, in the midst of which, his trusty valet came to inform him Miss Mansel had asked after his honour's health twice in the last half hour.

" Charming, delightful, kind Anna!" exclaimed Edwin.

The mirth which had exhilirated the countenance of Herbert in an instant fled.

" What," said he, scarce daring to breath, "who? Miss Mansel did you " say? Anna, is it her?"

" Ah,

"Ah, you know her then?" replied
the other—"Yes: who but she *could* have
"taken such entire possession of my soul?"

"I thought," said Herbert, "she was
"married?"

"Heaven forbid," answered Edwin,
"that any human being should dare to
"have a hope of the kind; no, she re-
"fused William Mordant and Sir Charles
"Stanley; refused them for me, Charles;
"I have stolen into her little heart; she
"must be mine."

"What, then, will you give up Miss
"Turbville?"

"Not so, neither."

"How will you, then, manage with
"Anna? you cannot think—"

"*Think*, I *know* she loves me, Charles,
"and by heavens I adore her; but I be-
"lieve we shall neither of us *think* it ne-
"cessary to have recourse to the dull
"beaten road of matrimony."

"Love, free as air, at sight of human ties,
"Spreads his light wings, and in a moment flies."

Mr.

Mr. Edwin, in the excefs of his rapturous ideas, ran on for fome time in this ftrain, and might have, uninterrupted, repeated all the poetry and common-place fayings the worn-out fubject of feduction could furnifh him with.

Herbert was too much abforbed in his own ideas (which were not of the pleafanteft kind) to attend to him; he was not, till this moment, fenfible of the ftrength of his attachment to our heroine; 'tis true he thought her engaged, and by this time married to the perfon of her choice; that, and that only, had prevented his attempting to render fuccefsful the firft ferious paffion he ever felt; but now that he found fhe was not only fingle, but in love with a man that meditated her ruin, his thoughts were in tumults?

Should he not endeavour to fave fweetnefs and purity fo captivating?

Were thofe elegant manners, thofe charms of perfon given her, then, in fuch profufion, to be the prey of vice? But how could fhe be faved? would a

woman

woman who could attach herself to a known libertine, thank him for an interference (rather impertinent than according to such ideas) friendly, and if so, what end would it anfwer, except involving their family in a quarrel, which would diftrefs his mother, and even bring the charge of ingratitude on himfelf? As he was confcious of many obligations to his uncle, he, therefore, for a moment, gave it up, and retired, under pretence of fatigue, pleading it as an excufe for not waiting Sir William's return from the houfe; but he could not leave Grofvenor-fquare without making his bow to Lady Cecilia; he accordingly was announced.

CHAP.

CHAPTER XXXIV.

The Pique.

THE crimsoned cheek of Anna would have told a very contradictory tale to that he had just now heard, had Herbert observed her; but a sensation resembling inward pride and resentment, added to the resolution he had just formed, and being prepared to see her, prevented that observation, or any other. After paying his respects to Lady Cecilia, he bowed with the cold indifference of a common acquaintance and no more.

Good heaven! what at that cruel moment were the feelings of Anna; her heart had fondly anticipated the pleasure of this meeting to Charles and herself; she could not, from all his behaviour, help indulging hopes of being dear to him; their parting

parting scene was ever present in her mind, the plaintive sound of his voice at that period still vibrated on her ear; and after all, was it thus they met! the pointed neglect, the cutting indifference, struck her with grief and consternation.

Too much confused to ask after his mother and sister, and scarce able to support herself, she took the opportunity of Lady Edwin's family inquiries to retire to her chamber, where a flood of tears relieved her swelling heart:—Ah, cried she! bitterly weeping, it was not to Mr. Mansel only, I discovered the imprudent, the presumptuous thoughts, my own folly too, too much encouraged; Herbert has perceived it, and despises me; he sees the forward girl is not to be trusted with the appearance of friendship; his looks, his manner, spoke a contempt I could not otherwise have excited.

But perhaps, continued the afflicted girl, the change in my situation has had this effect; and could Herbert, could he be the first whose behaviour should remind

her

her of her dependence on his family; was that the expanſion of his heart, the noble diſpoſition for which ſhe had ſo admired him: cruel Herbert, unhappy Anna; ſhe had created an idol in her own imagination, of manly beauty and goodneſs, her every thought had learnt to worſhip; he had barbarouſly torn away its amiable viſage, and ſubſtituted in its place the moſt frightful deformity; but ſhe would think of him no more, or if ſhe did, it ſhould be with the contempt ſuch caprice deſerved; ſhe would ſhew him, that true pride of conſcious worth, and integrity, was of no family, that it might exiſt, undignified by blood, unadorned by the gifts of fortune: ſuppoſe he had ſuſpected her imprudent affection, ſurely it could be no difficult matter to change that affection into ſcorn for one who could inſult a woman; for ſuch a change of behaviour, without the leaſt cauſe on her ſide, amounted, in her preſent imagination, to an inſult.

The value of Lady Cecilia's kindneſs to her now leſſened; ſhe condemned herſelf

for

for not taking Dalton's advice, and fixing
on a trade, whereby she might subsist, with
some little claim to independence: she had
lost all consequence with herself from the
moment she supposed she was of none to
Herbert; her heart sickened at the prospect
before her; she had written to Miss Edwin,
in her former stile, but had received no
answer, the sweet intercourse, and the
union of minds, that were to last their
lives, were already evaporated, and had
no more place in that lady's thoughts
than if they never had existed.

From the sentimental novelist of seven-
teen Miss Edwin was transformed into the
gay coquette of twenty; the hero of her
first romance only maintained his ground
in the variety of her ideas; Charles
Herbert was amiable, when over-run
with notions of love; she was ignorant
of almost every thing else; and now that
her fortune was a bait to every coxcomb
she became acquainted with, and her paf-
sion for admiration gave encouragement
to every fool to address her, still her cousin
was

was beyond compare preferable to any she
saw, and her pride was not a little hurt to
find his attachment to her by no means
what she had flattered herself.

Miss Turbville, her now bosom friend,
was the counter part of Cecilia; they were
educated together, and the formation of
their minds left to women who (interested
only by the price they received, and ignorant of the real accomplishments that render a young woman of fashion valuable,
to her own connections in particular, and
society in general) were gratified in making them acquainted with the superficial
knowledge, they themselves possessed.

Born to splendid fortunes, and never
contradicted in their lives, it is little to be
wondered their tempers were unamiable
as their manners; they both set out determined to be the heroines of sentimental
passions; but fine cloaths, fine company,
and fine jewels, with the very fine speeches
of a few as fine beaus, totally overthrew
the first soft system, and introduced an in-
ordinate love of dress, pleasure and admiration;

miration; fenfibility was banifhed, and the finer feelings were no more.

So that there was no confolation to be derived from the memory of Mifs Edwin's freindfhip.

Mrs. Herbert wanted refolution, and Patty, the amiable Patty, power to be of fervice to her; Dalton had plainly hinted fhe muft not think of living in his family Lady Edwin's protection was therefore her only refource, and there fhe muft conftantly fee the man of all others fhe wifhed to avoid; the advance of fpring promifed no alteration, as there was yet no talk of going to Dennis Place.

Lady Edwin at this moment fent for her to inform her of two things; one highly agreeable to her, was, that Mr. Herbert, his lady, and daughter, were arrived at their lodgings in Bond-ftreet, whither fhe defired her to go and welcome them; and the other that Cecilia, and Mr. Stanley's family, would be in town the following week.

Anna

Anna eagerly flew to execute the commands of her patronefs; Pattty wept with
joy, and Mrs. Herbert expreffed as much
pleafure as the gloom on her countenance
would permit; they had not yet feen
Charles, who came from Oxford to join
them; they returned with her to Grofvenor-fquare, and ftaid the evening.

. Mr. Stanley, guardian to Mifs Turbville, a moft worthy charaéter, was rejoiced
at the approach of the time that was to
free him from the care of a flighty girl,
whofe large fortune rendered her fo tempt-
ing an objeét; and therefore, fince the
mountain would not go to Mahomet,
Mahomet he faid, muft go to the mountain; in a word, he removed with his family to a ready-furnifhed houfe in Bur-
lington-Street.

It fignified nothing now to be fick; all
evafions were at an end; Edwin's honour
had been given to his father, to marry,
when he fo nobly provided for Mrs. Mitford: no excufe would be admitted by his
parents, and his ideas were fo full of the
charms

charms of independence, that when he could get the lovely Anna out of his head, he was rather defirous of being what he called' fettled.

But that was neither often nor of long duration, Anna returned with double force and with irrefiftible 'power, banifhing every. agreeable confequence of his marriage with another; he knelt, fwore, and vowed' in vain; fhe urged his obedience to his parents; to remember his family, fortune, and connections: and finally, declared her affections were engaged—Diftracted at this idea, he refolved to force a compliance from her; he now found it in vain to court; difappointed pride and vanity ftimulated a paffion that wanted no goad.

During the time of his feparation from Herbert, diffipation and vicious company had not done more towards corrupting his mind, than good fenfe and moral companions had effected to improve Herbert—the former felt that he refpected his coufin more, but loved him lefs for his fuperiority: notwithftanding his rational and polite

polite behaviour on all occafions, he had found him rather fhy of the confidence he was dipofed to place in him refpecting his defigns on Anna; and when he preceived he had impofed on himfelf, in his con-clufions of her partiality, he was pre-vented both by that and his own pride from revealing to him his difappointment, or future intentions.

Herbert on his part, now in the con-ftant company of our heroine, found reafon and reflection too weak to guard him from her fafcinating charms; yet, piqued at his firft behaviour, her whole deportment towards him was fo referved, fo cool, and fo diftant, that he doubted not Edwin was a favoured lover; he regretted a thoufand times he had not tried to make an intereft in her heart at Llandore—he recollected a variety of circumftances which might have convinced him fhe dif-liked Wilkinfon, but it was now too late to avail himfelf of thofe obfervations; for, befides that it would be difhonourable to his coufin, his own delicacy could

not bear to think of being fecond to fuch
a libertine, even in the heart of Anna;
yet he wifhed, fervently wifhed, fhe might
efcape the meditated ruin.

Thofe conflicts in his mind fo affected
him, that it injured his health, and change
of air was prefcribed: Mrs. Herbert would
gladly have accompanied her favourite, but
Lady Edwin wifhed her to ftay in town,
and advifed lodgings in its vicinity, or near
London, from whence he might ride occa-
fionally, or they vifit him; but he chofe to
return to Oxford, as foon (after he had
paid his refpects to Mifs Edwin and the intended bride) as poffible.

CHAP.

CHAPTER XXXV.

First Impreſſions.

MR. Stanley's family arrived in town the beginning of May; Mr. Edwin found his intended bride juſt the reverſe of what his heart approved in Anna: ſhe was, indeed, tolerably handſome, but vain, conceited, proud, and witty; had much ſmall talk, loud laugh, and large white teeth, her cheeks, as ſhe was very fair, ſhewed the rouge at the firſt glance, and her auburn brows were robbed of their beauty by a black pencil; her hair plaiſtered with pomatum and brown powder, formed a ſtrong contraſt to the clean cheſnut locks of Anna; in ſhort, if inſtead of captivating, ſhe had laid a regular plan to diſguſt, ſhe would certainly have ſucceeded.

But

But Mr. Edwin was too much a man of the world to suffer his sentiments to escape him inadvertently; it was his business to fall in love; and as very few men exceeded him in natural or acquired understanding, to which was added a graceful, handsome person, he was so fortunate as to render himself as pleasing to the lady as he affected to be charmed with her.

Cecilia was in the mean time playing off all her airs and graces, at her inanimate cousin, and vexed to death her pains were attended with so little success; her anger increased by observation not less galling to her pride than alarming to her jealousy.

Charles (pre-determined to be a close observer of Anna at the first interview of the intended bride and bridegroom) had no eyes or ears for any one else; he saw with extreme satisfaction the placid serenity of her countenance kept its unruffled, peaceful appearance; looks of curiosity were all the only ones she directed towards them; her face was the faithful index

dex of her mind, in her fine clear fkin every interefting change in her thoughts might be read, and the lovelieſt pair of eyes in the univerſe had not yet learnt any leſſons but thoſe of nature.

Cecilia faw and felt her fuperiority; felt it, accompanied with fcorn and envy— What whim could poſſibly induce Lady Edwin to keep fuch a thing about her !

She had been accuſtomed to watch the eyes of the men; it was not long before the ſtolen glances of her brother made another difcovery, which ſhe was reſolved ſhould be turned to uſe.

When they returned to Groſvenor-fquare, Miſs Edwin went with them; having fent her woman and baggage before; ſhe pleaded a head-ach as an excuſe for directly retiring, leaving Lady Edwin furpriſed, and Anna piqued, at the coolneſs of her behaviour, however, as neither thought it neceſſary to ſpeak their fentiments to each other, no obfervation was made.

Next morning Mr. Herbert and Mr. Mordant attended Lady Edwin's break-faft-table, which was at two early an hour for Cecilia; Charles came to take leave of the family, and Mordant once more to prefs his fuit with Anna; his intimacy in the Edwin family gave him but too many opportunities of witneffing the unex-ceptionable mind, as well as lovely per-fon of our heroine.

He brought from the gentleman who had the charge of him from his father a *carte blanch*; the time of his ftay in Eng-land was very near elapfed, and he for the laft time, now came to try his fate with the woman he loved. His intereft was warmly efpoufed by Sir William and Lady Ed-win; and finding Herbert was fo nearly related to the family, he alfo intreated his influence. Anna had before faid all that a determined mind could fay, and the prefence of Herbert was very unlikely to give a turn to her fentiments.

The reluctance with which Mordant re-figned his laft hope, engaged him till two o'clock;

o'clock, when, dreffed with the utmoft attention, in an elegant morning difhabille, in fwam Cecilia, brufhing her eyes over Anna, who refpectfully rofe at her entrance, bowed to the company, and fat down with a mixture of haughtinefs and contempt in her looks. Mordant directly applied to her for her intereft with her lovely friend—fhe was furprifed, could not divine who he meant—who could he mean but the charming Mifs Manfel—fhe had no influence.

Anna begged he would fpare her as well as the company; fhe affured him of her grateful remembrance of the honour he did her, which fhe acknowledged fhe thought her misfortune fhe could, not confiftent with her own notions of integrity, accept; her refolutions were unalterable. "Be-" lieve, me, Sir," continued fhe, with an amiable franknefs in her manner, and a modeft earneftnefs in her countenance, " if I could have returned the affections—" of fo worthy a man, it would have been " my pride to do it generoufly; you are " fo deferving, Mr. Mordant, I am fure

" you

" you will meet a heart more valuable
" than mine, that will require no inter-
" fering friends to do juſtice to your me-
" rit. God preſerve you, Sir," ſaid ſhe,
making him a graceful courteſy, and
immediately left the room. Mordant
then with a tender regret which affected
both Sir William and Lady Edwin, took
his leave. Miſs Edwin ſhrugged her
ſhoulders;— if a capital merchant would
not do, ſhe wondered what would!

Mr. Herbert now roſe to be gone; it
was in vain Miſs Edwin entreated his ſtay
a few days—ſhe wanted a beau—could not
poſſibly do without him—nay, he ſhould
ſtay. He declined all her invitations,
took his leave, and went from thence to
Mr. Edwin's apartment.

" Well, Charles, and what ſay you to
" my divinity? How do you like her?"
cried Edwin the moment he entered.

" I think her a fine woman, and hope
" you will be happy."

" 'Till death do us part, Charles,—do
" not forget that."

" But

" But what," ſaid Herbert, " do you
" think of her yourſelf? for that's the
" grand queſtion."

" Indeed, is it! But as it is a queſtion
" which, if anſwered ſincerely, will pro-
" duce a deviliſh rude one, it had better
" not be aſked. But come, Charles, as
" you ſay ſhe is a fine woman, and all
" that, if you will take her off my hands,
" you will oblige me very much."

Charles expreſſing no great *gout* to the
offered kindneſs, Edwin inveighed with
great bitterneſs againſt the folly and inſi-
pidity of both Miſs Turbville and his
ſiſter; ſwearing, that if it were not for
one ſweet hope, he would ſet off and
leave them to commit matrimony with any
one but himſelf.

" Ah! what a difference," ſaid he, " be-
" tween them and the angelic Manſel.
" Did you obſerve her abſolute lovelineſs,
" how, robed in her excellence, ſhe look-
" ed an emblem of ſweetneſs, innocence,
" and beauty? Upon my ſoul as I ſat
" (ſtunned with the tittering nonſenſe of

F 5   " my

" my intended wife)-at the other end of
" the room, when her coral lips opened to
" deliver, with grace and eafe, the fenti-
" ments of wifdom and propriety, the
" perfume of her breath feemed, to my
" adoring imagination, from that diftance
" to reach my foul. But come, Herbert,
" you fet off to-morrow; we will dine
" at a tavern to-day; where we will toaft
" the angel in half pints, until nothing
" of love, but the pleafure fhall have
" power to difturb us."

" Well," anfwered Herbert with a
faint fmile, " you talk it bravely; but
" you forget Mifs Turbville, is to dine
" here." " I leave her looking glaffes
" enow, and I'll fwear you debauched
" me," replied Edwin, " fo *allons*" taking hold of his arm.

We left Mifs Edwin with her father and
mother; the former, as I have faid, was
dotingly fond of both his children: Lady
Edwin's love for her daughter was greatly
leffened by her behaviour, which was neg-
lectful and often rude. She directly began
to

to wonder how her mother could think of taking such a girl as Anna about her; she was sure great inconvenience would arise from such a ridiculous piece of charity. Lady Edwin was astonished at the little ceremony her daughter used in speaking to her, and peremptorily bidding her attend to her own concerns, immediately left the room.

Cecilia, whose feelings, such as they were, had been too much for her to bear, before Herbert's departure, now cried out of mere spite. Her father tenderly inquiring into the cause of her affliction, was told she detested Anna; who was a proud, insolent creature, and who had the assurance, she was certain, to aim at ensnaring her brother.

Partial and indulgent as was Sir William to his children, he could not give way to so uncharitable an insinuation, but took the absent unoffending Anna's part with so much warmth, that his daughter flung from him into her own room, where, throwing herself on a sopha, she began to

vent

vent her anger on her woman, who, she declared, had purposely disfigured her head that morning, becaufe she knew it was her defire to look tolerable.

The woman, in broken Englifh, attempted to vindicate herfelf, and not without fome passion, which irritated her mistress to that degree, that she actually fcolded; and her voice founding all over the houfe, Anna ran towards her apartment, as did Mr. Edwin and Charles.

They found Cecilia, her eyes fwollen with crying, her face diftorted with anger, and her lips white and quivering in a perfect frenzy, and her woman, a foreigner, talking faft in her turn. Edwin burft into laughter at this fcene, which he told his fifter, wanted but a Hogarth to render it immortal; he fneeringly afked if she entertained herfelf often in this way! and immediately turned on his heel. But Herbert and Anna, actuated both by the fame fpirit of kindnefs, attempted to footh the fair vixen; their endeavours were not fuccefsful; she rudely bid them leave her apartment.

ment. The truth is, Anna waa fo much alarmed at what fhe heard and faw, and Herbert fo ftruck at this unexpected rencontre with her, and fo interefted at the difquietude in which he faw her, that, unmindful of Cecilia, his firft efforts were to calm her fears; and the fight of him in an attitude of the tendereft folicitude, imploring her not to be alarmed, one arm round her waift, the other fpread on his heart, while he hung over her enamoured, was not calculated to calm the raging tempeft in Mifs Edwin's dreffing room.

When at her repeated command they left her, fhe was on the point of difcharging her woman; but her peace was made, and fhe reftored to favour by a difcovery as new as unexpected.

CHAP,

CHAPTER XXXVI.

A Retrospect.

CECILIA's anger had been on the part of her woman quite unprovoked; it was not difficult for her to fee fhe was the victim of her lady's refentment to fome other perfon; her not thinking fhe looked well was a fure fign fhe wifhed fo to do; indeed this woman, whofe cunning was feldom to be exceeded, well knew Mr. Herbert had a powerful advocate in the breaft of Cecilia, and an indifferent fpectator might as eafily difcern that faw him with Anna off his guard, where all his wifhes lay.

This, therefore, was Mifs Edwin's rival; fhe was more, fhe was the indentical Anna, who fome years back had rival'd Madame Frajan, (for it was that very lady) in the affections of Colonel Gorget, the all accomplifhed;

plifhed; and who, as *fhe* had injured, it was impoffible *fhe* could forgive; befides the gallant Colonel, though now a Baron, a man of title, was no changeling. She had at different times paid her refpects to him, and as often received the compliment of one pound one, but never without regretting the lofs of his little flame. Two objects, therefore, immediately offered themfelves to her view,—interest and revenge;—what French *fille de chambre* could refift either?

Lord Sutton, but perhaps my reader may here accufe me of inconfiftency, having once introduced that gentlemau as a character univerfally defpifed, we fhould at our re-acquaintance find him graced with the favour of a virtuous Prince. But unheard of as it may feem for fo defpicable a character to be made a Lord, I entreat my readers to give me credit for the truth of his being fo. In truth the Colonel was very rich; fome trifling ocucrrences in his paft life, under the fignature of Gorget, were not fo pleafing to recollect

in

in their confequences; the name was fa-
mous, it was rather *too* well known :—he,
therefore, fome how or other by dint of
his intereft with Lady Waldron, got Baron
Sutton added to his confequence, whereby
in public matters Gorget was forgotten.

It was this very perfonage whofe addreffes were rejected by Lady Edwin for
her daughter, on account of his father's
obfcure original, and who found in her
fortune and connections ftill fuch attractions, that he had gotten Madame Frajan
into the family to forward once more his
applications, which, if rejected, he intended to try his influence with the lady for a
trip to Scotland; yet though fhe was young
enough to be his daughter, it did not follow that her perfon was, as he pretended, his ultimate object; Madame Frajan
knew the contrary, and if fhe had not been
fo certain of that, the improved perfon and graces of Anna would have decided her opinion. She had fome other
reafons, which will appear in the courfe
of this hiftory, to hate the fight of our
heroine;

heroine; fhe, therefore, fuffered Cecilia
to vent her rage, till again tears fupplied
the want of revenge.

It was then the fly frajan intreated her
pardon for having unwillingly offended
her, protefted her unbounded regard and
refpect, for fo fweet, fo amiable a lady,
which fhe flattered herfelf fhe fhould yet
be able to prove, and begged her for-
givenefs for a queftion that might appear impertinent, but which fhe fhould
give fufficient reafon for afking; and
with great humility begged to know
how long fhe had known the young woman Mr. Herbert feemed fo fond of?
The queftion was an irritation to the rage
of her foul—"Name her not," faid fhe
ftamping, "one houfe fhall not hold us:"
—this was the cue her woman wanted.

Nor need it, Madam, anfwered fhe: is
this then the Mifs Manfel Lady Edwin is
fo wrapt up in? an impoftor, a thief!—Mifs
dwin was all attention, her rage fubfided,
and the woman reftored to her favour, by
repeating to her the hiftory of our heroine;

fo mixed with facts, it was difficult to fe-
parate the true from the falfe : what the
refolutions formed on this occafion were,
will be feen in their confequences.

It happened that Lady Edwin was that
evening to have a grand rout, and Anna,
who was now perfectly acquainted with a
polite affembly, ufually did the honours
of it, receiving the company in Lady
Edwin's place; who was much better
pleafed to fit at cards, when Mrs. and
Mifs Herbert were of thofe parties. Patty,
whofe love to her friend, equalled her
deferts, generally kept pretty clofe to her.
—Herbert dining with Edwin, and Mr.
Stanley being engaged to be with Sir
William on family bufinefs, gave Cecilia
a pretence for requefting to be indulged
with the company of Mifs Turbville, and
dinner in her own apartment.

Mrs. Herbert calling in the morning,
begged Anna might go home with her,
which Lady Cecilia the more readily
agreed to, as they were to enter on
matters relative to the fettlement, and

it

it was not neceffary an uninterefted perfon fhould be prefent.

As foon as they got to Bond-ftreet, Mrs. Herbert, whofe aching heart always fat on her brow, left Anna and her daughter to themfelves: the intended wedding in the family, and the finery and fhew it would be attended with, for fome time engroff-ed their converfation; Charles and Cecilia naturally fucceeded: Patty obferved the great alteration in her coufin, and added, that fhe feared Charles would prove an ungrateful fwain, for fhe was fure that kind of woman was not the one for him; indeed, continued fhe, I have reafon to think he is ftrongly attached, but where, or to whom, I cannot tell; and if that fhould be the cafe, Mama will break her heart, as both families depend on its being a match; Lady Cecilia is fo good, fhe waves all thoughts of fortune, in confideration of the family intereft; and though my coufin has taken fuch a fool-ifh turn, you know fhe always loved Charles, and he her:—I thought, faid

Anna,

Anna, he had been her declared admirer ever since I have known them.

Why, as to that, answered Patty, I believe my cousin was rather too sanguine in her ideas of his love; however, I hope in God it will be brought about, for Papa goes on at such a rate, we had need have nobody else to vex us.—What reason have you to doubt it, my dear? why should you suspect he has an attachment?

While Anna asked this of her friend, the situation of her mind may be guessed: I'll shew you, said Patty, drawing a laylac breast- bow from her work-stand; I found this on his bed this morning; when he was gone out, Mama and I went into his room to look over some of his things, I caught it up: he returned very soon in a violent bustle; did not ask me for it you may be sure, but his man told Betty he wore it tied to a string round his neck, and had done so a long while; and,—looking in her friend's face at this period, she saw her pale and agitated; the alarm this gave, put the bow out of her head.

Anna

Anna was indeed ill; all that Mifs Herbert faid had affected her.—Poor Mrs.
Herbert, deftitute of any other confolation, robbed of all comfort but what centered in her fon, and his eftablifhment,
how could her felfifh heart give way to
wifhes that would counteract the only
hope of fo good a woman; even Patty
hoped in God it would be brought about.
How could fhe (was there no other objection) bring herfelf to give pain to the
gentle, the endearing Patty ?—but when
the bow was produced in evidence of her
fufpicion, fhe could no longer reprefs or
conceal her emotions; it was with difficulty fhe concealed her feelings; and,
unable to continue fo interefting a converfation, begged to go home: with
great reluctance fhe was fuffered to leave
them; and Patty engaged, if her indifpofition continued, to fpend the evening in
her apartment; if fhe was better they were
to meet in Lady Edwin's drawing room.
Without acquainting any body of her
return, Anna flew to her room the moment

ment fhe got to Grofvenor-fquare, and
having locked the door, as if her thoughts
could be feen, whifpered to her fond,
throbbing heart ;—if Charles Herbert loved
the owner of that bow, then was Anna Manfel the happy object of his attachment !

It was hers dropped, as I have related,
the week before fhe left Llandore. Pleafure filled her bofom, and joy throbbed in
her heart; fhe was now fure Charles
loved her; in that idea all thoughts of
forrow were banifhed: and, I muft own,
to the difcredit of our heroine, not one of
thofe very fine arguments fhe had made
ufe of to Edwin, and which might with
equal if not greater propriety, have been
urged to Herbert, prefented themfelves
to her recollection, fave the effect on his
mother's peace.

Her bow tied round Charles's neck,
was proof againft all the efforts of reafon
or prudence; and fhe indulged, for the
firft time, a certainty of being dear to
him: but whence that coolnefs on his
coming to London ?—No matter ;—if
                                        really

really cold to her, the ribband would not that very morning have been of such importance.

Thus, happily reftored to felf-confidence, fhe beftowed more than ordinary pains in adorning her perfon; for though Herbert had taken leave, as the two young men were to dine together, perhaps, in the courfe of the evening, they might drop into the affembly.

CHAP.

CHAPTER XXXVII.

The ungaurded Moment.

Lady Edwin knew not of Anna's return, till, fupremely lovely fhe attended in her dreffing-room, previous to going down to receive the company.

" You are fo charming to-night, Anna," faid Lady Edwin, " I defpari of prevailing on my daughter or Mifs Turbville to treat yon with common good manners: but let not that difturb you, the wedding will foon lake place, and Mifs Edwin will go for a time with her new fifter; I give you my word, the envy of little minds will never hurt you with me.'!

Anna gratefully thanked Lady Edwin for fo kind an affurance, and regretted her lofs of the young Ladie's efteem; faid fhe

could

could not charge herfelf with an act that ought to have that effect.

" Look, child, in the glafs," anfwered her patronefs, " you will fee a very good rea-fon, one that will find its way into the bofom of every young lady on my lift to-night."

On thofe happy terms, who could fore-fee that this was the laft night fhe fhould fpend under the roof of fo partial a friend ?

They entered the drawing-room in the greateft harmony: Mifs Edwin's return to town brought many young people of both fexes of the firft fafhion to the af-fembly; the great Welch fortune was an iuducement to the one, and the elegant ftyle they lived in entitled them to the ac-quaintance of the other.

The beautiful miftrefs of the ceremo-nies attracted every eye; a plain white luftring with black flowers, fancied in the moft fimple and elegant tafte, fet off her fine complexion, and her *tout enfemble,* was, indeed, ftriking; innumerable were the compliments paid at the fhrine of beauty by the few on whom it had power,

while the two fair friends in the circle
they fat, were exhibiting their witty talents at the expenfe of an innocent woman,
whofe heart was warm in every good wifh
towards them.

As fhe flattered herfelf, fo it happened; Edwin and Charles came in about
ten; the indifpofition of Anna, (which
they heàrd in Bond-ftreet) occafioned
their going into Lady Edwin's drawing-
room.

Edwin rallied her on her pallid looks,
and begged, for God's fake, fhe would be
ill again. Anna told him, fmiling, there
were eyes in the room that would not forgive him if his were diverted from their
proper objeĉt, direĉting him, by a glance,
from her fine eyes to Mifs Turbville's
party; but, reader, guefs, if it is poffible, her aftonifhment, when fhe faw,
playing with Mi's Edwin's fan, moft fu-
perbly dreffed, her old friend Gorget, now
Lord Sutton.

Had a gorgon faced her, the effeĉt
could not have been ftronger: her colour
changed;

changed, and her tremour was fo vifible, that Herbert, who was near, obferved it, and begged fhe would fuffer him to attend her into the other room for air. Scarce knowing what fhe did, fhe complied, and he had the happinefs of fupporting in his arms, fome moments after fhe got out, the woman he adored.

In this fond moment, unguarded by caution or prudence, he befought her to lean on him ; her hands were, alternately, preffed to his bofom, and he addreffed her by the tendereft appellations :—this behaviour alarmed and difpleafed her; and having drank a glafs of water, they both attempted to recollect their fcattered thoughts. Herbert, however, had gone too far to recede; he therefore intreated her pardon for a difcovery her fituation had wrung from him, and eloquently pleaded the force of a paffion he neither expected nor wifhed to conquer, though he knew it was hopelefs.

Anna, who could interpret this to nothing but her dependent fituation, an-

fwered

swered haughtily, he was perfectly right, and immediately left him. More wretched and more confirmed in her love for Edwin than ever, he returned to the company pale and dejected; and only staid to make a passing bow to Lady Edwin and the young ladies.

CHAPTER XXXVIII.

Disgrace.

ON account of her indisposition, Anna sent an excuse to her patroness, who returned a friendly injunction on her to be careful of herself: she passed a very restless night, an unaccountable dread seized her spirits, though innocent of a thought of offending any human being; she feared she knew not what.—Just as she was leaving

ing her chamber, a packet was given her, directed to Mrs. Herbert, by Lady Edwin's woman, with orders to deliver it immediately.

This command was as extraordinary as it was new; neverthelefs as it was her part to obey, fhe walked to Bond ftreet. Mrs. Herbert was not up, and Patty was gone, on a fudden whim, to Richmond, with Charles, who made it in his way to call on a widow fifter of his father to dinner; fhe fent up the packet with defire to know if there were any anfwer? After waiting an hour, Mrs. Herbert came down; but inftead of the cordial, warm, reception, fhe had been ufed to from that lady, a courtefy hardly perceptible was all—fhe fat down.

Poor Anna could not fpeak at firft; but when fhe could articulate, begged, for God's fake, to know the meaning of fuch a dreadful folemnity; Mrs. Herbert pulled out the packet, and, opening it, looked at her very earneftly, and demanded

how

how long fhe had affumed the name of Manfel?

Nothing had ftruck Anna, at the firft appearanct of Mrs. Herbert, but that fhe had difcovered her attachment to Charles; her countenance, therefore, brightened up at this queftion, confcious of having nothing to blufh at in the change of her name, fhe immediately told her.

" Did you wait on Mrs. Melmoth?"

" As to waiting on her," Anna faid, " fhe fhould have been proud to render " her any fervice in her power; but never " had attended her as a fervant."

" You left her in difgrace, child, I think?" " I am to this, moment, ig- " norant what my offence was."

" There," faid Mrs. Herbert, with a folemn fteady voice, " is half a year's " penfion from Lady Edwin. Mrs. Man- " fel did ill in introducing you to our " family; I am forry I ever knew you; " I am, at this inftant, concerned more " than I wifh for you; have you any " friends in London?"

Lady

Lady Cecilia herfelf had not more laud-able pride than Anna. Perfectly innocent of any one action that could prejudice thofe ladies fo much againft her, and hurt equally by the matter as the manner of her difcharge, fhe retreated from the offered money, and to the queftion of, " Had fhe " any friends?" anfwered, " It is not, " madam, for an orphan, who has no " connection, natural or acquired, to " boaft of her friends; few in a more ele-" vated ftation abound with them; it is " enough that you, madam, muft be cer-" tain I have enemies—you perhaps know, " though I do not, to what length thefe " have carried their unprovoked malice. " If I have deferved to be difcarded in " this manner, I have no claim to the " money you offer. When I am told of " what I am accufed, I will try to acquit " myfelf; till then, I have only to pray " for yours and the family's happinefs."

This faid, with an air of injured pride and innocence, fhe was going, but recol-lecting herfelf, " afked if fhe was to re-

" turn

" turn no more to Grofvenor-fquare, how
" fhe was to get her things?

" They will be fent where you direct,"
anfwered Mrs. Herbert.

On which fhe fet down with her pencil.
as the only place fhe could recollect; the
inn where the Brecknock ftage put up,
on the arrival in town. And leaving the
houfe, called a hackney coach, threw herfelf into it, and bid the man drive to
Whitechapel, where the ftage from Dalton's village ftopped; being juft in time,
fhe immediately proceeded to Layton.

The whole tranfaction had been fo fudden, and fo unexpected, that fhe could
fcarce credit her fenfes, or believe fhe was
now on the road to Layton. One comfort, indeed, offered itfelf—fhe had not
left Charles Herbert behind. On recol-
lecting and putting together circumftances, fhe concluded, fhe muft owe to
Colonel Gorget's ill will this new misfortune; but what could provoke him to
this inveterate perfecution of her fhe
could not imagine, except it was the
dif-

disappointment of his wicked attempts on her when quite a child; yet the time was so short, since she had parted with Lady Edwin, on such very cordial terms, she could not conceive the method he must have taken to work so quick a ruin; she thought and thought again, and the coach stopped at Dalton's door before she had pleased herself in her conjecture.

When Dalton saw her and looked in her dejected countenance, he exclaimed, " What, the bad money returned."

This salute in her present situation and state of mind was too much; her tears moved Mrs. Dalton, who received her very kindly, and begged she would not make herself uneasy; that she would be always welcome there. " Ay, ay," said Dalton, "for a while, so she shall, but it " is time she knew how to get her bread." This was her own opinion; but how it was to be done, was the point. Spite of herself, some latent hopes would arise that she might, one day, be united to Charles, and in that case, would the proud Cam-

brians

brians of his family ever acknowledge a mantuamaker or a milliner? What, then, could she do? She could think of nothing else, and Dalton still harping on a trade, Mrs. Dalton said, that as Peggy was now out of her time, and in business for herself, Anna might try a little with her first. To this she made no objection, when she should arrange her little matters; during which period, she told the greedy Dalton, she would pay for her board; this Mrs. Dalton positively refused.

Anna sent for her things, which were left, as she directed; when they were delivered at the door, her heart sunk; she had hoped either letter or message would have accompanied them, that would give some light into what had been her offence, or, perhaps, an invitation to return: two or three days elapsed, but no news came from Grosvenor-square, or (what was worse) from Bond-street.

CHAP.

CHAPTER XXXIX.

The Correspondence.

THE fourth day Anna received the following billets:

" When laſt I ſaw and pleaded the cauſe of love, awed by your frowns, and ſilenced by your peremptory commands, I feared I muſt for ever drop the rapturous hope of poſſeſſing the lovelieſt of women; but you will now, perhaps, hear that from reaſon, which paſſion durſt not plead. Any ſettlement in my power to command is yours; family, friends, even country, ſhall be ſacrificed to the wiſhes of my charming Anna, whoſe name, in future, ſhall be that of her adorer, if ſhe chuſe to aſſume it. Write to me, I beſeech you; I need not put any other ſignature

G 6   than

than that of the man who moſt loves you : you will recollect whom.

BILLET THE SECOND.

" Madam,

" It is with difficulty I traced you ſo as to receive your addreſs : the tranſient view I had of you at Lady Edwin's aſ- ſembly, gave me hopes I ſhould have an opportunity of offering you any ſervice in my power, as the friendſhip I felt for you at Melmoth Lodge is ſtill freſh in my memory.

I was much ſurprized, on inquiring of that lady, this morning, to hear you was diſcharged the family. I do not mean an impertinent inquiry into the cauſe, but I deſire Miſs Dalton will honour me with any commands that may be acceptable to her, in the power of, madam,

Your moſt obedient

Humble Servant,

SUTTON."

BILLET THE THIRD.

" Ah! my dear Anna, what can your Patty fay to comfort you under fuch cruel mortification! You need not tell me you are innocent; how little do thofe know you, who can think otherwife: I long to fee you, but am forbid by all the family; poor mama bears the blame from every body—how he came by it I do not know, but my coufin has a direction which he fays will find you, if it does, pray write to your

P. H.

" P. S. You muft direct to me under cover to Mr. Edwin; he is your ftaunch friend and advocate."

Indignation at the two firft of thefe notes gave way to pleafure at the laft; tears of gratitude filled her eyes—"Sweet friend, dear girl," flowed from her lips; fhe re- folved to anfwer it immediately, for two reafons; one was, fhe wifhed to oblige

Mifs

Miſs Herbert; the other, ſhe longed to know what ſhe could be accuſed of—yet how could ſhe approve of the means of correſponding which Patty propoſed; as little as ſhe knew or ſuſpected of the ways of intrigue, it was plain, directing to Miſs Herbert, under Mr. Edwin's cover, would give him a pretence to viſit her, an honour by no means deſirable in his and her preſent ſituation; for did he not profeſs to love her, a profeſſion injurous to the peace of the lady he was about to marry, as well as inſulting to her own honour; yet how elſe to write to her friend, ſo as to prevent her laying under the diſpleaſure of the family? And if ſhe did not write, would not her ſilence give Patty an impreſſion of her ingratitude, it was impoſſible ſhe could deſerve; could ſhe otherwiſe find out of what crime ſhe had been accuſed, or by whom, or could ſhe by any other means ever know any thing of Charles? The laſt thought decided the point, and the following ſhort note was diſpatched :

" To

" To Miss Herbert.

' May you never, my deareſt friend, by being in diſtreſs, experience the kind of joy your note gave me; yet I do not approve of this means of thanking you—Of what am I accuſed? only tell me that— I cannot wiſh to engage my friend in a correſpondence which muſt be blameable but that one favour, till better times, is all I aſk of my Patty, who will forgive the declining any farther uſe of Mr. Edwin's friendſhip, to her ever grateful and affectionate

A N N A."

Having written this, Anna ſet herſelf in earneſt about thinking of future ſubſiſtence; although Dalton's harſh expreſſions hurt her, yet ſhe could not in juſtice diſapprove them; ſhe ſaw his large family, all of whom were now getting their own livelihood by the laudable exertions of induſtry—Peggy, the eldeſt, lived with them, and contributed to their general ſupport; ſhe had a great deal of work about the vil-

lage,

lage, and it being now fummer, when moft young folks, in the middle line of life, have what new cloaths they can afford, was very full of bufinefs—the affiftance of our heroine was therefore no lefs timely than acceptable, and her natural tafte being good, fhe very foon took all the trimming and ornamental part on herfelf; added to this, her late refidence in the great world, enabled her to inftruct Mifs Dalton in the fafhions moft in vogue, whofe fame in confequence became fo great, that the ladies, that is to fay, the tradefmen's wives, who, either by the fuccefs of induftry, or a fpirit of prodigality, had country houfes, began to employ and reccommend her to each other, fo that bufinefs came in very faft, and Dalton, confequently, grew more civil.

But the latent difeafe of the mind depends not on either fucecfs or difappointment in the common occurrences of life; and pride had too great a fhare in Anna's compofition to render her eafy in fuch a fituation.

Lord

Lord Sutton's letter had excited no other emotions than thofe of hatred and contempt; fhe was fure his ill offices had a fecond time robbed her of her protectrefs; and fo rooted was her bad opinion of that nobleman, that fhe dreaded no evil but what fhe imagined would originate with him: his letter was therefore toffed into the fire with the moft perfect fcorn and indifference—and here it may be neceffary to remind my reader, in Mifs Edwin's chamber fcene, which dif-covered Anna to Frajan, the former was too much taken up to obferve the latter; her attention was divided between Cecilia and Herbert; or, if fhe did obferve her, fhe had not the flighteft recollection of her perfon during the few minutes fhe was in the room, a circumftance that will not appear ftrange, if we recollect Frajan not owning herfelf married, the appellation merely as a French waiting woman in all genteel families is Mademoifelle only, and Anna being always in Lady Edwin's apartments, it was next to impoffible, during the fhort time fhe continued in Grofvenor-fquare,

venor-fquare, after Mifs Edwin's return
from Bedfordfhire, that fhe could have
any perfonal knowledge of her attendant;
fhe could form no conjecture of the author
of her difgrace in the Edwin family that did
not point at his Lordfhip.

Many returns of the poft having paft,
and no letter arriving from Mifs Herbert
—at length, wearied out with expectation,
and mortified with continual difappoint-
ments, fhe wifhed to turn her thoughts to
things within her own abfolute reach:
and though confcious fhe had taught
Dalton's daughter more than it was poffible *fhe* could learn from her, yet, tired
with the father's continual teazing, her
confent was obtained to be bound for two
years to the bufinefs, and he joyfully applied to an attorney to draw the inden-
tures; however, before this matter could
be completed, it was entirely put a
ftop to.

They were at work one morning in a
room appropriated for that purpofe, when
an uncommon rattling of coach wheels under

der the window, and a loud ráp at the door, excited their curiofity; but what was Anna's furprife, to fee Lord Sutton alight from a fuperb carriage; indeed it took from her the power of fpeech; and while Peggy was making a thoufand conjectures concerning the object of this vifit, from a perfon in a coroneted coach, Anna was abforbed in her own ideas, wholly unable to comprehend the meaning of fo unwelcome an intrufion.

Lord Sutton was fhewn in, and Dalton inftantly recollected in the vifage of the noble Lord, him wbo had made four years before, fuch alarming inquiries after Anna, felt guilty and abafhed, and doubting from his fplendid appearance the day of reckoning was come—Trembling and pale, it was with infinite difficulty he could mufter up courage to afk the ftranger's bufinefs.

Lord Sutton, proud only of his rank, riches, and fplendour, found his vanity highly gratified by the vifible confufion of the poor parfon, who he fuppofed was confounded at his grandeur.

After

After enjoying fome moments with the appearance of the moft ftately indifference, the confufion he excited, he changed at once the haughty Peer into the artful infinuating fycophant, made many apologies to Mr. Dalton for his intrufion, which, he faid, was occafioned by his defire to ferve a young perfon under their protecrion, who, though fhe had been difcarded by a relation of his who had taken her when very young, was, he prefumed, too well educated to be capable of being ufeful to an inferior ftate of life, and too handfome to be fafe in fuch an age as this from the purfuits of the licentious.

Mrs. Dalton, whofe heart had nothing wrong about it but what fhe derived from her hufband, without the leaft guile in her own compofition, was in raptures at this kindnefs; fhe was ready to worfhip him, and heaped praifes in the warmth of *her* heart, which his told him *he* could never deferve—but whatever happy prefage this good woman's credulity gave him, he was not lefs furprifed than vexed, to obferve the

hufband's

husband's silence (for he had not spoken since the first salutation) proceeded, from some other cause than mere respect for his Lordship. He, therefore, addressed him with praises for his humanity to Anna, so profuse, that Dalton, conscious how little merit he could plead on that account, felt himself more hurt than gratified; and callous as was his conscience, turned the many compliments paid him to an ironical meaning. Undetermined, therefore, in his ideas, he interrupted his guest, by asking him bluntly, if he had not seen him before?

Lord Sutton, although exceedingly disconcerted, was too great an adept in hypocrisy to suffer it to be seen. With an affable smile he commended the retentive memory of the preacher, which he supposed must be of great advantage both to himself and his flock, and answered he was not mistaken, that he had felt the same compassion then for his ward he yet retained, and that in consequence he had made those inquiries, which were of great trouble to himself, without (he spoke

it

it with regret) ferving the young lady,
as he, Mr. Dalton, pofitively denied any
knowledge of her, a conduct he muft own
quite inexplicable to him. "And pray,
" Sir," faid the ftill doubting parfon,
" who may you be?" "My name, Sir,
" perhaps (at leaft if you have read the
" hiftory of the fuccefs of our armies
" abroad) you may have heard—it is
" Gorget—I had the honour to command
" the army in the Eaft Indies; my poor fer-
" vices his majefty has thought proper to
" reward with a title; Lord Sutton, at
" your fervice."—The room inftantly became too fmall; the cringing Dalton, reaffured no danger was nigh, immediately
adopted the utmoft fervility both of fpeech
and countenance; while his wife, in endeavouring to clear away her litters, threw
every thing into diforder. A Lord was a
being in whofe prefence it was impoffible
for them to fit; nor could all his condefcenfion prevail on either of them to take
a chair, till he arofe and abfolutely refufed
to refume his feat except they favoured him
with their company.   He

He then artfully begged to confult them
on the means likely to be of fervice to
Anna, declining their firft offer of calling
her down. Dalton, who never for a moment loft fight of his own intereft, explained to his Lordfhip her prefent fituation, and what he had planned for her
with his daughter; adding, that as his
Lordfhip was fo very good and charitable,
if he wohld recommend them to work for
the great ladies of his acquaintance, it
might be the making of both.

Sutton, with all his caution, could hardly
keep his temper at this propofal; he had
in the cafe of Frajan taken large ftrides to
place a French waiting woman of infa-
mous principles, in attendance on a young
lady of fafhion and character; but to take
on himfelf to recommend a couple of honeft young women as mantua-makers,——
what could the fellow mean? Neverthelefs
he feemingly acquiefced—one only objection ftruck him; he faid, he doubted
whther Anna was not more qualified for
the ftation fhe had juft left; he feared fo

fedentary

fedentary a life would not fuit her education; and as to their daughter, it
fhould be his ftudy to evince his refpect
for the parent, by his friendfhip to the
child; he would recommend *her*, whether
Anna continued with her or not.

This fet the matter in a new light. His
Lordfhip was the beft judge; he had only
to fignify his pleafure to them, and they
would obey to the utmoft in their power all
his injunctions. Mrs. Dalton then repeated the motion of calling Anna; his
Lordfhip bowed his affent. She imem-
diately carried this joyful news to our heroine, not doubting but fhe would be in
ecftafies; but the cold and contemptuous
reception of the great friendfhip that
waited her acceptance, together with her
abfolute refufal to go down, almoft petri-
fied the poor woman; *what* not go down
to a *Lord*, not accept of *his* offered fer-
vices? What would this world come to?
" Indeed Anna," continued fhe, " I never
" till now could credit what Mr. Dalton
" has often feen in you; your pride
                        " will,

" will, as he fays, I am afraid, come down."

Anna, piqued at this fpeech, fat filently to her work; but on Mrs. Dalton's ftill urging her to go to his Lordfhip, fhe fuddenly threw it down, and faid fhe would follow her. This fhe did from a determination to let Lord Sutton fee fhe was not the dupe of his artifice, and farther to convince him fhe was not likely to become fo. Accordingly Mrs. Dalton announced her intention, and in fhe went. Tranfient as was Lord Sutton's view of her at the affembly, it had left her image deeply rooted in his heart; the beautiful girl of fourteen he had never ceafed regretting the lofs of, and the vice which reigned predominant in his foul, was continually placing her innocence and budding charms before him in a light too acceptable to his libertine principles; but when the fame beauty, innocence and fimplicity again met his eyes, adorned with every grace and accomplifhment—when the fweetnefs and charms of her countenance ftruck him, more captivating from their maturity, he felt, what he had till this moment been unfusceptible of, a fincere paffion; which to gratify he was determined at all events, be the expenfe or trouble what it would.

When the fair victim, he now refolved never to lofe fight of, appeared before him, when he again beheld her, a tremour feized his guilty frame; he hefitated and faultered, but endeavouring to conceal by a low and refpectful bow the diforder of his countenance; he paid her compliments on her improvements, which from any other perfon might have flattered the vanity of a young woman: but here refentment, at the unprovoked ill offices and recollection of the bafe advantage he had taken of her unprotected ftate at Melmoth Lodge, were too ftrong to be forced by a plaufible appearance or fine fpeeches; and the humble fituation in which fhe was, fo far from mortifying or abafhing her, only ftimulating her pride; with a haughty air fhe demanded his bufinefs.

This was a reception the proud, yet mean, Lord was not prepared for; and

again

again his admiration of the lovely object before him deprived him of all his guard and fortitude; he however attempted to glofs over both his letter and vifit, by alledging compaffion and humanity as his motives for both.

Oh! ye divine fources of every comfort to the diftreffed, how were ye here proftituted to the worft of purpofes!

Anna thanked him; but as fhe could fubfift independent of his offered kindnefs, infifted on declining that and every favour from him. Your youth, Madam, faid he, and inexperience of the world you are to live in, is with me an apology for this return to the warm effufions of friendfhip and good will. I was once, it is true, fo unfortunate as to offend the purity of your ideas; but affure yourfelf, Mifs Manfel, I was then, as now, incapable of meaning you injury: you muft allow for the prejudices of education; for the free manners in a man the world not only difpenfes with, but even approves. I have been, I do not deny that *I am*, a free liver with refpect

to

to your fex; meeting, therefore, alone, a pretty girl, I might, without a farther thought, be tempted to fteal a few kiffes.

The indignation and fhame which filled the heart and countenance of Anna at this varnifhed excufe, were too apparent not to ftrike him with conviction of her incredulity; but he had other ends in view than fpeaking to her; it was at the Daltons; they he had the fatisfaction to fee, eagerly credited his profeffions, and as eagerly condemned the conduct of their ward to fo great a man.

The liberties he had taken, with the infult he had offered her, he was very confcious would not bear the excufes he had made; but he depended on her modefty and delicacy for her filence. He was right; the injured innocent was now in her turn abafhed and confufed; it was but for a moment however, her natural pride and integrity, reanimated by the recollection of the diftrefs this man had brought on her, enabled her, with a rejecting motion of her hand, to tell him, if the world were fo in-

dulgent

dulgent to fuch actions as he had been guilty of, and fuch principles as he poffeffed, it was the fitteft place for him, and the moft unfit for her to figure in; fhe therefore begged he would return to it, adding, fhe was too fenfible of the obligations fhe was already under to him, particularly *late ones*, to wifh to encreafe them; and, courtefying, contemptuoufly, withdrew.

Every word and action increafed the anger and aftonifhment of the Daltons; who, from the moment he announced himfelf a Lord, fet themfelves down as made people; he already fancying himfelf in a fat living, fhe with delight anticipating the aggrandifement of her family through his recommendation, and having herfelf no idea of wounded delicacy or infulted honour, nor fufpecting the open, candid, humane perfon before them of plotting the ruin of innocence, could not comprehend from what madnefs or folly Anna could thus refufe fuch defirable and advantageous offers of friendfhip. The rude anfwers fhe returned deftroyed the caftles they were building

and

and left traces of difappointment on their countenances much more vifible than on that of their vifitor; he knew how to take advantage of this difpofition in them, and with an air at once of forrow and chagrin, lamented the obftinancy of Anna, that put it out of his power to gratify his own wifhes in ferving her. However, Madam, faid he, turning to Mrs. Dalton, though it is hard to meet unthankfulnefs where we know we deferve gratitude, fuffer me to recommend this poor ill-judging young woman to your farther protection; and fince fhe refufes my good will, permit me to requeft you will accept this trifle towards the expenfe fhe muft be to you, and promife not to make her acquainted with it. Having faid this he fhook hands with the Parfon with great apparent cordiality, and ftep-ing into his carriage, was no fooner out of fight, than eager to examine the contents of a purfe that felt fo very refpectably, Dalton and his wife retired to a little inner room,——twenty guineas was a fum fuf-

ficient

ficient to give force to weaker arguments than thofe ufed by Lord Sutton; it fet his in an unanfwerable point of view, it eftablifhed their notions of his generofity, and revived the hopes they had formed from his acquaintance.

After much deliberation it was agreed they fhould join in perfuading Anna to write to fuch a noble friend, afk pardon for her ingratitude, and implore his returning favour. Accordingly they went, and having extolled his goodnefs both to them and her, got the affiftance of their daughter, and all three befet her with arguments and entreaties, by foothing and threats, by fair means or foul, with equal fuccefs; fhe was too fenfible of what was right, and her principles were too juftly founded to fuffer her judgment to be biaffed where her honour was concerned; fhe faw with grief he had found the weak fide of Mrs. Dalton, and the wicked one of her hufband; and that in confequence fhe muft expect to be farther perfecuted.

But as rapes, and carrying off by force, fo generally related in modern novels, had

not

not been part of her readings, and as they are things that do not often happen in real life, she apprehended no other dan-ger from him; indeed his age and debili-tated conftitution were fecurities from thofe evils; she therefore contented herfelf with hopes to hear no more, than from the Daltons, of a man for whom, and for no other perfon living, she felt a real hatred, and continued her negative to all their arguments without affigning to them her reafons. Perhaps she may be accufed here of a blameable referve; but true delicacy and true virtue even feels the ftrongeft repugnance to think of, much lefs repeat actions hoftile to their tenets; and it is to thofe who really pof-fefs that character a kind of humiliation to admit they have ever been infulted.

But the grand account of a life devoted to injury and deceit practifed on the in-nocent and unwary, was now to be fettled on the heart of Lord Sutton.

The elegant deportment, the charms of our herroine, appeared the more irrefiftible

from

from the difficulty that attended his purfuit; his foul long rendered callous by a
continual guard over himfelf, and the gratification of almoft every inclination he
had fuffered himfelf to indulge, its faculties weakened, and his perfon fo debili-
tated and infirm, that he was become an
antidote to that fex who had been his
former prey, now received impreffions that
deprived him of reft and peace—the more
he reflected, the more ardent was his paffion—he curfed his own precipitancy at
Melmoth Lodge, and firmly refolved to
let no thought or look efcape him now to
alarm or increafe her diflike, of him; all
his thoughts were bent on the means of
attaining the poffeffion of what feemed
neceffary to his exiftence. How to com-
pafs this defirable point, did not appear fo
eafy as he wifhed; but to give up any
defign once formed, or leave one ftratagem
of fraud or hypocrify uneffayed, would
have been as new as the paffion which
now filled the mind of Lord Sutton.

His arts, in conjunction with Frajan,
had robbed her of every friend but thofe

(if they might be called fo) fhe was now
with; the power of wealth, joined to the
artifice he was mafter of, he had no doubt
would be all the force he wifhed with.
Dalton and his wife: but what method
he fhould purfue to render Anna propiti-
ous to his defires, was the thing that moft
puzzled him.

It was neceffary to fubdue her pride as well
as virtue; to do this fhe muft become dependent on him—his friendfhip muft be indifpenfably neceffary to her fubfiftence.

Again the idea of folely devoting to her
his charming perfon revived, and with it a
refolution immediately to pick a quarrel
with a widow of pleafing perfon and large
family, whom poverty had induced to liften
to his addreffes, and accepted the place of
miftrefs of his town houfe in the room of
a high bred lady who had left him in
company with a difcarded groom: his own
pride had made him drefs this woman out
with great elegance; but as it required art,
as well as attraction, to keep alive the appearance of paffion in the noble Peer, and

as

as this lady was not an adept in her calling, he felt no kind of concern for her or hers; and the moſt ſhe could boaſt of was a kind of ſplendid miſery.

CHAPTER XL.

An odd old Man.

ANNA in the mean time attended to the buſineſs, though Dalton ceaſed to teaze her about the articles; it was impoſſible in a ſmall country village ſo near the metropolis, when the chief inhabitants were the wives and daughters of tradeſmen who could not exiſt without a country houſe, of which number there were many at Layton, ſuch a figure as hers ſhould be unnoticed; ſhe ſoon be-

came

came the subject of curiosity, of admiration, and of scandal. Who and what can she be? She is very handsome—she dresses too elegant—is too accomplished and genteel for a mantuamaker—she has certainly been somebody's mistress. A coroneted coach with a glaring suite of attendants, stopping above an hour at the door, with a gentleman only in it, afforded subject for censure and confirmation. At the assembly of Mrs. Bibbins, the same evening, a very pretty, delicate young man, designed by nature for a retailer of gauze, but jumbled by chance into a brandy merchant, as he was called, assured the ladies, in the softest lisping tone imaginable, that he was certain she had been in high life, for that he had seen her in a box at the Opera, when he and his sister (a young lady then present) were in the gallery; which was confirmed with the additions of Miss's being sure she was one of those bold women, viz. a kept one—she knew her again the moment she saw her. This matter

settled,

settled, not a person in company, save *one*, but had penetration enough to discover the most innocent countenance that ever graced the creation, to be one of the abandoned cast;—this was *a woman.*

Mrs. Wellers was the wife of a merchant who had retired from trade with a decent competency, leaving an only and deserving son in possession of his all, which was employed in procuring him a footing in a bank of great reputation, where he was at first placed as cashier: his sobriety and attention insured him that success, and impowered him to make those returns to his worthy parents, their noble confidence in him deserved: he married a woman of plain person and manners, with an excellent heart, and large fortune: they had several children; and Mrs. Wellers saw the goodness of her own disposition, and the universal good will she bore the whole human race, richly rewarded in the particular prosperity of her own family; entirely at peace with herself, and satisfied with the uprightness of her own

mind

mind and actions, she was the last to believe any reports that could injure or dif-
tress an individual, and the first to seize
on every occasion of vindicating an absent
person.

Mr. Wellers had taken very much lately
to frequenting Mr. Dalton's chapel, and
though he had no crimes out of the common frailties of human nature to repent of
himself, he was a great encourager of religious practises in those who had: the
Doctor himself did not take more pains
with his hearers than Mr. Wellers; and
often his house was subject to guests of his
spiritual acquaintance, not very acceptable
to his wife; notwithstanding, the sweet-
ness of her disposition made her give way,
with great good humour, to those little
whims in a man she had thirty-four years
entirely loved and honoured; and sometimes she had been prevailed on to go to
chapel with him.

It was here our heroine had struck her;
not indeed in the light the rest of the company had seen her; she felt herself prepof-

fessed

feffed in favour of that beauty and fimplicity fhe thought fhone in her countenance;
and having in the courfe of employing
Peggy Dalton, been frequently in company with her, fhe immediately, and with
no little warmth, defended the condemned
Anna; I wifh I could fay with fuccefs, but
the fiat was gone out; to be convinced
by arguments fupported only by candour
and benevolence, againft fuch glaring
crimes as youth, beauty, and poverty,
would be proof of a weak and yielding mind,
few people chufe to be guilty of; and to re-
cant an opinion formed on fuch ftrong
grounds, a condefcenfion not to be expected.

The good Mrs Wellers was not inti-
midated by her want of fuccefs; her thorough knowledge of life, and perfect
practife of politenefs, rendered her the
leader of every thing elfe in the village;
but fhe had not power to enforce her own
candid and generous fentiments; yet as,
when once a character was attacked, fhe
never gave up her point while a poffibi-
lity remained of defending the abfent, fhe
feldom

feldom failed in the pleafure of finding herfelf rewarded for her perfeverance, by fee-
ing, with the affiftance of a little time
and patience, every doubt removed, and
innocence cleared up.

It is much to be lamented, that notwithftanding this is a circumftance which daily
happens, it is often protracted by fome un-
lucky accident, till the calumniators are
either removed from the fpot, or themfelves
in the fame calamity they fo unmercifully
inflicted on their fellow creatures, otherwife
fomething like fhame might poffibly operate for the general advantage of mankind.

When this worthy woman left Mrs.
Bibbin's, fhe began to revolve in her own
mind the feveral circumftances fhe had refufed to credit in the courfe of her vifit.

There was certainly fomething more in
the appearance of Anna than in the common run of young women in her fituation: her drefs, fo much fuperior to Dalton's daughters, either wholly contradicted his affertion, that he had brought her
up on charity, or if that were fo, fpoke a

myftery

myftery in which fhe found herfelf interefted, and refolved to take the firft opportunity of finding out.

Anna, confcious of no caufe for fhame,
faw herfelf an object of general obfervation; but as fhe had always been fo, though
from different motives, it had no other effect on her than reftraining her from walking out, when a recefs from work would
have allowed her that recreation.

It happened, that the next morning
after Mrs. Bibbins's rout, Anna was furprifed by another vifitor, as unexpected
and undefired, though not quite fo odious,
as Lord Sutton: this was Mr. Edwin;
he was fhewn, or rather walked, into
the room, where fhe was at that moment
in converfation with Mrs. Wellers; her
crimfon'd cheek immediately directed the
eyes of that deferving woman to the gentleman, in whofe countenance the greateft
fatisfaction appeared, and whofe glances
at our heroine ill accorded with his affir-
mative, on being afked whether fhe
might congratulate him on his marriage.

Mrs.

Mrs. Wellers made an offer of going; but Anna, who happened to be quite alone, and not chusing to be left with Edwin, intreated her stay, under pretence of expecting Peggy Dalton, tho' she in reality knew she was gone to town, and would not return till evening. Curiosity added weight to her request; and the lady, to the visible displeasure of the gentleman, was reseated.

He told Anna they were just returned from Bedfordshire; that he had suffered, with great anxiety, any constraint that prevented him from waiting on her; assured her he had shared the mortification *she* had received from *his* family, and that all he could command was at her service.

This very open declaration from a man who acknowledged himself a bridegroom, staggered Mrs. Wellers' good opinion of our heroine, more especially as it was received in silence.

After a pause, Anna inquired of the health of Lady Edwin and her daughter.
The

The latter, he told her, was with Mrs. Edwin, the former gone to Wales.

"Accompanied, I fuppofe," anfwered Anna, "by Mrs. Herbert and her family." An affenting bow called up another blufh.—Mrs. Wellers had now almoft given up the caufe of poor Anna; when fhe was moft agreeably furprifed, after a fecond paufe, to hear her addrefs her vifitor in a very folemn manner.

She told him, however honoured fhe might be, by his condefcending to take notice of a perfon who had been fo contemptuoufly difmiffed his family, fhe muft beg leave to remind him, that the more deftitute and friendlefs fhe was, the more it behoved her to take care of what only fhe could call her own, which was her good name—"Far, Sir," continued fhe, "be it from me to infinuate, that "the fon of my benefactrefs, a married "man, a bridegroom, would wilfully do "any thing that could lead to a depri- "vation of that moft invaluable trea- "fure: but you muft forgive me, Sir, "if I remind you of the utter impro-

"priety

" priety of a young woman of my rank
" receiving visits from a person of yours,
" in the predicament in which I now stand
" with your family: should any officious
" tale-bearer but mention the circum-
" stance of your being here this morn-
" ing, would it not justly offend ladies,
" for whom I have a sincere veneration?,
" —Pardon me, Sir, (for he was eagerly
" interrupting her) the conclusion drawn
" might no less affect your peace than
" my character; I therefore must beg to
" be excused seeing you, if at any future
" period you should make Layton in
" your way."

This plain dealing was by no means acceptable to Mr. Edwin, who gave Mrs. Wellers a look of displeasure, and intreated Anna to favour him with five minutes conference.

The request was refused as eagerly as asked—He insisted on it—She was immoveable.

Great as were his chagrin and disappointment, he did not chuse to discover

half

half what he felt; he, therefore, rising, said he would take some more favourable opportunity of waiting upon her with his message from Miss Herbert.

" Have you then, Sir, any message from " her , and could you be so cruel as to " detain it so long?—Alas! I feared she " had forgotten me," answered Anna.

The starting tear as she finished the sentence, thrilled the heart of Edwin, who only made use of Miss Herbert's name to gain his point of speaking to her, but a farther thought now presented itself to him, as a stratagem by which he might have her fully in his power: he, therefore, in a cool, resentful manner, wished her a good morning ; said he saw she was engaged, but hoped to be more fortunate in the next visit he had the honour of paying her.

Anna would now have wished to detain him, but could not prevail on herself to make any farther attempt.

When he got to the door, his servants had retired to a neighbouring alehouse, which the convenience of an adjoining
shed

shed entitled to the name of an inn—Edwin, at no time a good master of his servants, now being mortified, and his hopes founded on Anna's situation so entirely repressed, was in no humour to forgive this stolen refreshment; he swore he would break the rascals' bones; and seeing an elderly decent person on the opposite side of the way, looking earnestly at him, asked if he had seen his scoundrels?

The person, unaccustomed to such a laconic address, gruffly answered, he was not used to look after scoundrels.

Irritated at his words, and more at his manner, Edwin fiercely threatened to horsewhip him into better manners.

The man, as much a stranger to a drubbing as the fear of one, instantly crossed the way—Edwin, in the pride of riches and prosperity, (forgetting that a breach of the peace might subject a man of the first consequence to inconvenience) was as good as his word, and handsomely made use of his whip.

The

The neighbourhood, alarmed at such an outrage, to a person who unfortunately was no small favourite of the poor of the place, came to his assistance, and our bridegroom was soon in the safe custody of a blacksmith, constable, and his assistant, a collar-maker.

The person he had insulted, to his infinite surprise, proved one of the wealthiest men in that part of the country; one, who was above a pecuniary compensation, and whose rage at the affront as well as injury would admit of no palliation.

An action at law he knew would be a means of putting the assailant to an expence which he could not suppose would be an object to the young gentleman: he therefore wisely determined to take him before a magistrate, and prosecute him for the assault.

Edwin, whose understanding was exceedingly good, and whose knowledge of the laws and customs of his country had not been, even in his tour, neglected, saw the disagreeable predicament in which

his

his paſſions had involved him, and endeavoured to aſſuage the reſentment of
Mr. Beatly, but in vain: before a magiſtrate he ſhould go, and give ſecurity to anſwer his offence at the next quarter ſeſſions.

Ineligible as this ſituation was for a
man of faſhion, there being no remedy,
he got ſome of the bye ſtanders to hunt
out his ſervants, not wiſhing to return to
Dalton in ſo diſgraceful a ſituation. The
men were ſoon found, and it was lucky
for them his wrath had met with ſuch a
ſet down; he bid them follow him, with
an execration delivered between his teeth,
which was productive of a freſh offence,
as his vindictive adverſary immediately
took witneſs of it, in order to oblige him
to pay the penalty for profane ſwearing.
Never was poor young man of gallantry
treated with leſs reſpect or ceremony, during their walk to Mr. Juſtice Trap's; the
iron gate being unfolded by a ſervant in
livery, who was in Scrub's true explanation of his ſervice, his twin brother;
one part, indeed, of his buſineſs exceeded
the

the Herculean labour of Farquhar's original, fince to the duties of gardener, coach-
man, footman, and groom, was added
that of clerk and prompter to his mafter,
although the fees of office were not part
of his earnings, a hardfhip under which
he was obliged to be content for many
reafons, the principal of which was, his
having been a tradefman in the village at
the time his mafter worked as journeyman
with a barber in the fame place; and, by
misfortunes it was neither in his power to
forefee nor prevent, gradually reducing in
his circumftances in the fame progreffion
as the fortunate Mr. Strap had rifen, and
at this period having a wife and family
on the fpot, the generous juftice had
taken him in the above feveral capacities
out of charity, for which he allowed him
eight fhillings per week.

By this grey-headed fervant or clerk,
then, our party was ufhered into his worfhip's prefence.

Salutations, not, indeed, of the moft
friendly kind, paffed between his worfhip

and Mr. Bently who told a plain matter of fact tale, producing witneſſes to ſupport his charge. Mr. Strap had, therefore, nothing to do but aſk the delinquent whether he had any, and what bail to offer, as if he had not, a mitimus, which Arnold was ordered to produce, muſt be filled up.

Edwin was much better acquainted with the power of Strap than he was himſelf; and having ſufficiently cooled ſince he offered the offence, begged to ſpeak with both gentlemen without other witneſſes; he found great difficulty attending this requeſt, Mr. Juſtice Strap being a very placable perſon, and by no means capable of giving offence where it could be returned, and Mr. Bently ſtill ſmarting under the weight of his daring breach of the laws of ſociety.

At length, however, the favour was granted, after the precaution on the ſide of the magiſtrate, of a whiſper to Arnold, when having told his family and connections, he made every acknowledgement
poſſible

poſſible for a gentleman, and offered any
ſatisfaction for the affront; this *ecclairciſſe-*
ment had a very different effect on his two
auditors. The juſtice forgot to enforce
the neceſſity of the mitimus, in the very
great reſpect he profeſſed for the perſon
who was to have been the object of it;
he proteſted were it him, he ſhould rather
look on the little paſſionate ſally of ſuch a
man, as a piece of good fortune than
otherwiſe, as it was the means of putting
it in his power to confer an obligation,
where it was the higheſt honour to receive
one, and he made no doubt but Mr. Bently
would be of his opinion.

" Not quite ſo faſt, good Mr. Juſtice,"
anſwered that gentleman, " ſpeak for
" yourſelf; you and I ſee this matter very
" differently; you, I perceive, are inclined
" to pardon in Mr. Edwin, actions that
" would ruin one of his footmen; as to
" the good fortune of a horſewhipping
" from a great man,—why I wiſh you
" had it with all my heart; but *this* is
" not the *firſt* time you and I have been

" of contrary opinions; if this *man* (for
" I will not call him *gentleman)* were of
" lefs confequence, his offence would be
" lefs likewife; and were it not in his
" power to injure fociety as much by ex-
" ample as precept, the particular af-
" front offered *me,* fhould not excite an
" unforgiving fpirit.

" But here comes a great man, and,
" like *your* honour, (bowing to Edwin)
" he happens to be out of humour about
" a wench, a hare, a card, the turn of a
" die, or fome fuch *important* matter:
" well, he chances to meet fome infigni-
" ficant fellow, whofe head being happily
" free from any fuch impreffions, is quiet-
" ly following his concerns on the King's
" high road, thinking nor meaning injury
" to any created being; poh, fays the
" great man, *you* fhall not tread the fame
" ground, breathe the fame air, look erect,
" or wear your beard like me; but why,
" and like your honour, (bowing again to
" Edwin) not becaufe I am better, older,
" or

" or wiſer, but becauſe I am *richer* than
" you.

" That may be an incontrovertible rea-
" ſon with you, Mr. Juſtice; but I am,
" as I dare ſay you think, an odd, obſti-
" nate old fellow; and it gives me great
" pleaſure juſt now to ſtand in the me-
" dium between the overbearance of the
" rich, and the rights of the poor. If
" my groom, pleaſe your worſhip, being
" a luſty young fellow, had laid an old
" man by the heels, I would have pu-
" niſhed him legally, or ſent him into
" confinement as an inſane. Mr. Edwin's
" front, to be ſure, has nothing wanting
" *in it*; but, neverthelefs, I ſee there no
" ſtronger plea to excite compaſſion than
" in Dick Grovers."

" Compaſſion," anſwered Edwin ſcorn-
fully, " your age—"

" Ah, generous youth, would thou
" hadſt before remembered it," as ſcorn-
" fully retorted Bently.

" I ſee," ſaid Edwin, " every conceſ-
" ſion but adds to your inſolence." Then

addreffing himfelf to the magiftrate, he mentioned the difficulty he was under about bail, as it was in the county of Effex, where he could not recollect an individual he knew.

The civil Mr. Strap undertook to take care of every thing of that kind, ordering Arnold to ftand up for one, and the conftable for the other. This being adjufted, Mr. Bently retired, and Edwin acknowledged the politenefs of the Juftice, and inviting him to Portman-fquare, was, by him, moft obfequioufly attended to the outer gate.

He left Layton with the moft mortifying reflections; fincerely did he condemn the paffion, by which he had put himfelf in the power of fuch a low-bred fellow, as he called Bently; and bitterly did he curfe the pride of her who occafioned it, not that he minded the law, but the ftory might get wind. What excufe could he make for vifiting Anna at all? Some terms it was neceffary he fhould keep with his family, and the little remains of refpect

he

he felt for his parents, who he knew would be much hurt at the idea of his being carried like a felon before a petty magiftrate, not a little difturbed him.— This train of reflections brought him back to his fervants, both of whom he ordered to be difcharged the inftant he got to town; they *then,* bound by no intereft nor awed by any fear, told the whole affair in the fervant's hall; and before fix, it was a fettled thing among Mr. Edwin's domeftics, that their mafter kept Mifs Manfel.

Mr. Dalton and his family, I have faid, were out, the day Edwin was at the village; they were gone, by invitation, to dine (where my reader will not expect to find them) with no lefs a perfon than Lord Sutton; there the fplendour of the houfe, magnificent fervice of plate, quantity of fervants and rich liveries, opened a new world never feen or fufpected before by that family; they were firft fuffered to wait in view of riches that appeared endlefs, till their ideas of the owner were

accom-

accompanied with an awe which increafed
with each new thing that appeared : and as
their waiting was protracted for no other
reafon than to give them impreffions fuit-
able to his purpofe, his entrance into the
room, with the moft placid fmiles upon
his countenance, cordially fhaking hands
with Dalton, and faluting his wife and
daughter, almoft turned their brain.

He immediately entered into a very free
converfation with them, adopting their
manner of difcourfe, and gave them a
dinner abounding with every delicacy
the feafon afforded; to which were added,
the various fuperfluities, which, at the
command of the rich, are taught to counteract the law of nature, by bringing the
bloom of fpring to deck a winter table,
and fpreading it in fummer with the hoary
appendages of winter. The moft coftly
and delicate viands were handed round in
a plenty and profufion, of which the
humble vifitants knew not the name; and
the water, vainly, though with the moft
fervile refpect offered to people, who were

ftranger

ftrangers to the cuftom of ufing it at table.—A defert fit for the entertainment
of a royal gueft followed.

Wonder and admiration kept filent
thofe for whom fo much pains had been
taken, and the table would have been
cleared without its being touched, but for
the great attention and folicitude of the
noble Lord, whofe polite recommendation of each different fruit and confecti-
onary drew them out of their wonder into
a more subftantial enjoyment of the
things before them.

When the fervants withdrew, having
impreffed his guefts with equal ideas of
his riches, politenefs, and generofity, he
artfully, by inquiries into their income,
and expreffing his furprife it was fo fmall,
threw out hints of many different ways
by which it might be enlarged.—Suppofe
Dalton's return to the church, as he had
connection, and, indeed he flattered himfelf, intereft with fome of the firft people,
in whofe particular line prefentations lay;
in the mean while, till fomething could

I 5

be

be done, he muſt inſiſt on their accepting an annuity from him; he could not bear ſo amiable a woman as Mrs. Dalton ſhould feel an inconvenience it was in his power to prevent, or ſo worthy a man as her huſband want any friendſhip he. could command. And having made ſure his way, he now ventured to mention their ward; he lamented that her pride and obſtinacy deprived him of the pleaſure of doing her a two-fold ſervice, that of aſſiſting herſelf, and of relieving them from the burden of ſupporting her; he aſked them whether they could tell on what occaſion ſhe had been diſmiſſed Lady Edwin's family.

Mrs. Dalton's anſwer was conſiſtent with truth; ſhe lamented Anna's obſtinacy in refuſing his favours, which he was grieved ſhe ſtill perſiſted in, though ſhe had no friend elſe in the world, as to be ſure, though ſhe pretended to be ignorant of the cauſe by which ſhe had loſt the protection of the Edwin family, it was to be ſuppoſed that Mr. Manſel would adopt their ſentiments.

Dalton,

Dalton, I have informed my reader, wanted not cunning or penetration; the depravity of his own principles made him clearer fighted than his wife; the latter ever confided in the appearance of candour, and believed all proteffions made her, with the moft credulous fimplicity.

Sutton appeared to her more than mortal with fuch powers, and fuch inclination to be of fervice to individuals; fo little pride, and fo much humanity blended in one character, were fo different to any thing fhe had fancied of a great man, that not a fufpicion to his difadvantage could poffibly find its way into her mind.

Not fo her hufband—the attention of Lord Sutton, fo conftant and unfolicited, his extraordinary generofity, the beauty of Anna, and character of the man, which was too notorious to be a fecret to any who chofe to enquire, were ftrong reafons for clofe obfervation: and he had no kind of doubt, but his Lordfhip's views

on Anna were more perſonal than he wiſhed
to be known.

He conſidered himſelf in no degree an-
ſwerable for the event; he wiſhed heartily
to get rid of a young woman on whom he
could not look without feeling a kind of
ſhame and ſelf reproach, which by long
habit had changed to a hatred of the object, that cauſed ſo diſagreeable a ſenſa-
tion; without taking from his own family
their all, it was now impoſſible to do her
juſtice. Lord Sutton could not, therefore, more fervently wiſh to get poſſeſſion
of Anna, than Dalton to be freed from
her. Theſe thoughts, however, had too
evil a ſource to be communicated to his
wife; paſſive obedience and non-reſiſtance
he had long taught her, but her morals
were yet good: avarice only found its
way into her mind; from his conſtantly
preaching how neceſſary money was to
the ſubſiſtence of children ſhe fondly
loved.—He had, indeed, been as particularly careful to guard every ſenti-
ment of his own which would leſſen her

confidence

confidence in his religious practise from her as from the rest of the world, which, from her difposition was eafy enough to effect : he, therefore, encouraged her great encomiums on Lord Sutton; nor was he himfelf backward in his acknowledgments; concluding with a hint highly pleafing to his Lordfhip, that if Anna continued her wicked unthankfulnefs of heart, he fhould not only difcard her himfelf, but expect to be repaid the expenfe he had been at on her account.

. This Chriftian refolution exhilirated the countenance of Sutton, and gave the wifhed for explanation of the principles of the profeffor of religion :—they parted in mutual good humour, his Lordfhip prefenting Peggy with five guineas for the expences of the day.

CHAP.

CHAPTER XLI.

A new Friend.

WE left Anna in the best hands—Mrs. Wellers, whose curiosity had carried her to Dalton's, found herself less satisfied, but more interested by what had passed during Edwin's visit—A train of reflections, the most melancholy and depressing, took such entire possession of my heroine, at the departure of that young man, that Mrs. Wellers had twice bade her good morning, before she was sensible of any thing but her own gloomy ideas.

After some time, however, her eyes met those of that Lady, bent on her with a mixture of surprise and compassion, that at once confused and affected her:—the silent tear stole down her glowing cheeks: —again recollection of past events crowded on her imagination;—her agita-

tion

tion increafed—fhe turned pale;—a ficknefs overpowered and rendered her an object truly affecting to the humane Mrs.
Wellers, who affifted in foothing and re-
covering her, with a moft delicate attention,—avoiding even to afk the caufe.
When Anna could collect her wandering
ideas, fhe refpectfully apologifed for the
trouble fhe had given the lady, and
thanked her for her kindnefs with an air
of the ftrongeft dejection.

Mrs. Wellers feeling herfelf more and
more interefted, declared that fhe would by
no means leave her to fuch evil company
as appeared to have taken poffeffion of her,
but infifted on taking her home to dinner,
and fhe fhould continue with her till the
family returned from town.

Anna would have gladly excufed herfelf from accepting her confiderate invitation.—The evil company alluded to, were
thofe fhe moft wifhed to indulge;—but
Mrs. Wellers was too preffing to be refufed—and as fhe knew the Daltons paid
great court to that lady, not only on ac-

count

count of her bufinefs, but of her influence,
fhe concluded it would be improper to
rifque affronting her by a refufal; and indeed the whole of this Lady's conduct had
been fo kind, it was againft her own feelings to do it;—accordingly Anna accompanied Mrs. Wellers to her habitation
above a mile from the village.

Mr. Wellers was not at home, fo that the
day was fpent with no other company;
and the beauty and fweetnefs of our heroine
in the courfe of it were found to be her
leaft perfection:—the education fhe had
received, of which, in her fituation at Dalton's, hardly any traces were difcernible,
now, in the fociety of a well-bred, fenfible
woman, was difplayed with additional luftre,
as it was wholly unexpected.

The eafe and politenefs of her behaviour
and converfation, the modeft difplay of her
abilities, and the rectitude of her fentiments, equally pleafed and furprifed her
new friend:—who (though fhe longed to
know by what accident fo lovely, and fo
accomplifhed a creature became an inmate
with

with people so very inferior, in every difcernible point, as those with whom she
lived) forbore any kind of inquiries.

She had indeed gone to Dalton's with
that intention, having no apprehensions of
giving offence, where the offer of her ser-
vices would so fully compensate for any
transient mortification. The journeywo-
man of a mantuamaker could not be
thought to carry much sensibility about
her:—but when she had spent one day with
Anna, her respect increased with her lik-
ing, and she intreated, at parting, often
to be favoured with her company.

During her walk home, the reflections
which had been interrupted in the morning, returned.

Miss Herbert, had totally, she feared, de-
serted her, till Edwin's hint of a message
had awakened hopes too acceptable to be
conquered—She regretted incessantly the
not giving him the desired conference—
Yet the billet, which she was convinced
was his, was certainly an indispensable reason for refusing it—but could a moment
have

have been of confequence——, yes, one
moment would have expofed her to the
reproaches of her own heart——*What* did
that fond heart hanker after?

Mifs Herbert was forbid correfponding
or honouring her with notice;——and had
fhe not declined receiving any favour from
that young lady, through the medium of
Mr. Edwin?——Could there be now a juft-
fiable reafon for altering her mind?——Alas,
no! the latent caufe of her involuntary regret fhe wifhed to conceal from herfelf.——
They would now be going to Wales;
what would Mr. Manfel think of her being
difcharged from a family, on whofe native
juftice and benevolence all who knew
them depended? She had not yet written
to that good man; how could fhe bear to
wound his heart by a tale of diftrefs he
could not relieve?——She had hoped to
have heard from Lady Edwin how her
misfortunes could have deprived her of
fo valuable a protection; and there were
moments in which fhe refolved to write to

that

that lady—but a certain pride of confcious rectitude and innocence forbade it. " Why " fhould I fink," faid fhe, " lower than " my fortunes ? If I had injured Lady " Edwin; if I could accufe myfelf of one " thought or act towards her, unaccom- " panied with affection and refpect, no " humiliation could be too great for fuch " an offence ;—but as it is, Mifs Edwin " fhall not feed her family pride with my " folicitations." But fhe would write to Mr. Manfel; he would give her fome information refpecting thofe to whom her heart involuntary turned. She had hitherto fupported herfelf in the idea that her prefent fituation was unknown to young Herbert; but now fhe found the wedding had taken place with all the fhow and parade Lady Edwin from the firft de-. figned—fhe could not doubt he was there, and acquainted with her difgrace.

Indeed if he was not, his correfpondence with his fifter was regular and punctual, and it was not probable, an event fo remarkable, as that of her being fo fud-

denly

dently difcharged from the family, fhould
not have been communicated by her to
him, more efpecially when Mifs Herbert
was fo good as to intereft herfelf in her
fate—" Alas!" cried fhe, weeping, "he
" no longer remembers the wretched
" Anna; or perhaps thinks of her with
" contempt—But what have I done; how
" have I deferved this cruel reprobation?
" Deareft Patty, have you too given up
" your friend; do I live only in the me-
" mory of my perfecutors and enemies;
" is there on earth fo forlorn an out-caft?
" Oh! if my parents could look down on
" the grief of their unhappy orphan,
" would they not lament the fate that
" preferved my exiftence, fince it is fo
" marked by continual diftrefs; fince
" every friend on whofe compaffion my
" orphan ftate has found a claim, is either
" prejudiced in my disfavour, or torn from
" me by the ruthlefs hand of death."

The tears which accompanied thofe reflections, were freely indulged during her
walk home; fhe entered Dalton's houfe
with

with a pale face, fwollen eyes, and a heart funk with defpair.

CHAPTER XLII.

Loft Reputation.

To her infinite furprife, Anna found not one friendly countenance; Mrs. Dalton looked on her with anger, her hufband with rage; and Mifs Peggy, who was, in her own eftimation, a foot taller, for the compliments of the day, with contempt.

Wholly innocent of a htought of giving offence to any of them, fhe could form no reafon for their ill humour, but having fpent the day with Mrs. Wellers. She related that lady's vifit, and her ftrong invitations to accompany her home;—but fhe was foon undeceived, and the grief. that before occupied every thought, gave
way

way to amazement and indignation, on being accufed by Dalton in the loweft terms, of receiving the vifits of a married man, who had left her in the heat of a quarrel, and wreaked his fpite on old Mr. Bently, who had charged a conftable with him—that the reafon of her being dif-charged Lady Edwin's family was now evident—that her imprudence had rendered her the talk of the place, and involved him and his family, on whom fhe had no claim but charity, in her difgrace.

Anna, poor and diftreffed, was proud and innocent—fuch a charge, from a man who ought to have protected her from infult, was too much for her little fhare of philofophy to difpenfe with; her heart, which had been foftened by her fenfibility, now became ftout in her confcious integrity—With a calm determined voice, though her whole frame evinced her inward diforder, fhe demanded to know who it was that dare accufe her of the horrid things his unfeeling tongue had uttered.

" Inno-

"Innocent creature," retorted he, provoked that his anger had not ftruck dumb a perfon fo dependent on him; "*You*, "then, in the whole village, are only ig- "norant of what has happened; can you "deny Mr. Edwin's having vifited you in "our abfence—by accident, to be fure— "we will believe of that as much as we "can.

"I can no more, Sir," anfwered Anna, "underftand your language than I can de- "velope your meaning. Mr. Edwin did "certainly, as you fay, vifit me this morn- "ing; but why it fhould expofe me to "fuch indelicate treatment, you only can "tell."—"What bufinefs had he with you, "Anna?" faid Mrs. Dalton. "Will you "fay, he came with the knowledge of the "ladies of the family?" "I have not faid "that," anfwered fhe, "nor anything con- "cerning his coming; his coming was as "unexpected as unwelcome to me; Mrs. "Wellers was here when he came, and was "fo good as to ftay the whole time he "continued. I know nothing of the quar- "rel

" rel you hint at; I had spent the day at
" the Hill, but had I not so good a witness
" of my conduct,, it would have been no
" cause of regret, as the last thing I could
" expect was to meet accusation from those
" who are bound in consideration of their
" own credit to have vindicated me from it."
And here the recollection of what would
have been Mr. Mansel's conduct on such an
occasion, striking with the vivacity which
generally accompanies the actions of people of warm passions, she told Mr. Dalton, that, " since he knew so little of her,
" she would no longer trespass on the *cha-*
" *rity* he upbraided her with, but instantly
" return to Mr. Mansel, were it only to
" clear herself with respect to the motives
" that induced Lady Edwin to part with
" her."

This declaration by no means suited the
Daltons—if Anna left them, what became
of all the advantages their sanguine hopes
had almost brought to a certainty from
Lord Sutton? Peggy, indeed, though a
very ordinary girl, had been so highly flattered

tered in his compliments to her, that she
gave it as her pofitive opinion his friendfhip for them was fixed: indeed, why
fhould it not? What was there in Anna fo
particularly interefting which they could
not plead for themfelves with equal right?
Mrs. Dalton joined her in faying, fhe
thought Lord Sutton too good a man to
think worfe of them for the fault of Anna;
but added, her being an orphan, and
friendlefs, were ties which they had not.
Dalton was filent but took a private refolution to inform his Lordfhip of what happened the next day; and and in the mean
time defired his wife to follow Anna up
ftairs, and endeavour to foften what had
paffed; inwardly refolving, if it were not
Lord Sutton's defire fhe fhould be detained,
to repeat the affront, that fhe might indeed fet off in anger, and rid him for ever
of a perpetual fource of difguft.

Mrs. Dalton found her in a fituation
that difarmed every idea of anger her hufband's intelligence excited, for it was him
who was told, and communicated to her
the events of the day. Unlocking her trunk

in order to pack up her clothes, the firſt thing that preſented itſelf to her was a letter written by her depaited friend; the tender and generous ſentiments it expreſſed, the praiſe beſtowed, and the maternal love it contained, now wrung her heart. "Oh, "my dear and only friend!" cried ſhe, in a tranſport of grief, "Why, why are you "for ever loſt to me? How little does "it now avail me to have cheriſhed your "inſtructions, to have made your perfect "life the model of my actions. In the "wide world have I not a ſingle friend to "do me common juſtice, Could you have "thought your Anna would have lived to "be charged with infamy?" In thoſe ex‐clamations on her knees, the open letter in her hand, and her face bathed in tears, ſhe was found by Mrs. Dalton, whoſe good nature immediately co-operating with her huſband's deſire, induced her to comfort and ſooth her, who ten minutes before, ſhe had joined in reviling as the worſt of criminals. Anna was ſoon appeaſed, but not happy: to find herſelf the talk of the place as a woman who received im‐
prudent

prudent visits, cut her to the soul; and having inquired into the particulars of the affair, she found the reflections on herself
proceeded from what the servants had in
their cups said at the inn, who made no
scruple of attributing her discharge from
the family to a criminal affair with their
master; and that now the wedding was
over, they supposed she was to be taken
into keeping.

A scandal, so void of the least foundation
was the more provoking, as there was some
part of it out of her power at present
to confute. Uncertain what step to take,
and depressed beyond measure in her spirits,
she could only lament her unhappy lot,
and depend on the justice of Providence to
clear her fame; making, however, a strong
resolution never to see Mr. Edwin again
on any pretence whatever—no, not from
Miss Herbert—and to take the first opportunity of leaving Mr. Dalton's. Her zeal
for returning to Mr. Mansel now abated;
could she think of burdening that good
man with her afflictions? Could she wish to

involve

involve him in difgrace and diftrefs ? What
to her was now the opinion of the Herberts ? If, as the fervants alledged, fhe was
difcarded on account of Edwin, Charles
would not be the laft to hear a tale fo in-
jurious to her honour; his fifter had certainly given her up—that indeed ceafed to
be matter of wonder when it was confidered fhe too muft have credited a ftory fo
calculated to deftroy every bias of an uncorrupted mind.

Confcious that he had actually paid her
his warm addreffes at the very period he
was entering into a matrimonial contract
with Mifs Turbville, fhe now reflected
bitterly on her own want of difcernment;
fince from that circumftance it was evident,
however difguifed under the appearance of
refpect and delicacy, his views had the a-
bandoned end fo openly declared in .his
billet. She regretted not acquainting Lady
Edwin, at the time, with all that had paft;
but her regret now came too late—her
good name, that invaluable jewel of a woman, was hurt—innocence alone could not
clear

clear her character, and she had nothing else to oppose against the calumny so recently excited by the folly and imprudence of Mr. Edwin; sad as those reflections were, they were continually uppermost in her thoughts.

To return to Mr. Mansel she could not bear—to stay at Dalton's was worse; unknowing and unknown, what hope could she entertain of making more fortunate connections than those which had cost her so dear? Yet she was resolved to try; and for this purpose seriously began to search in her mind for some clue to guide her through the labyrinth before her.

Mrs. Wellers was the only person with whom she held common conversation out of Dalton's family, since she had been at Layton; to her she resolved to apply, and, if necessary, to open her whole mind. In this disposition she walked to the Hill the next morning; but not having the good fortune of meeting her at home, she left word she would call the next day.

K 3　　　　　　　CHAP.

CHAPTER XLIII.

Contains Things of great Importance.

DALTON went, as he proposed, to Portland Place; if he wanted confirmation of his suspicions before, the change of countenance in Lord Sutton would have been sufficient,—rage, jealousy, and sorrow, were alternately, visible in a face, never tolerable, now absolutely hideous.

A volley of imprecations startled Dalton, and the furious Lord hardly could restrain himself from manually rewarding his intelligence; the affrighted Parson wished himself out of the house, and lost, in fears for his personal safety, all hopes of future advantages; however a little thought on one side, and patience on the other, explained the sentiments of both.

Lor

Lord Sutton made an apology for his warmth, which was very readily accepted by Dalton; they proceeded, therefore, to bufinefs with equal eagernefs, and it was agreed, the noble Lord fhould call, by accident, next morning at the reverend teacher's houfe, to try, aided by the advice of her friends, to prevail on Anna to move out of the way of feduction, or if it was too late for that, to preferve her from the farther evil confequences of fuch an atrocious crime.

Lord Sutton's humanity carried him ftill farther; Mrs. Edwin was a charming woman, and deferving a better fate; he felt for her—to refcue her from the mifery of difcovering the infidelity of her hufband, and, at the fame time, to remove from him the temptation of continuing to injure fo fine a creature, were, as he affured Dalton, what he had moft at heart; his praifes were echoed with all that fervility opulent vice ever receives from indigent finners; and thofe fentiments which owed their origin to the moft abandoned motives,

tives,

tives, attributed to the divine emanation
of Chriftian benevolence and good will to
the perfon he wifhed to deftroy.

When Dalton had taken his leave, and
Lord Sutton retired to his library, freed
from the impertinence of obfervation, dif-
tracting as the idea was, it was but too
probable that the fweet prize he had fo
long meditated obtaining, was now for
ever torn from him; the pangs of jealoufy
this thought gave, convinced him of what
he did not like to believe, that his heart
was now really attached, and that, *mau-
gre* all that vanity could urge, it was
without the leaft hope of return. To that
excefs he adored Anna that he now regretted he had not offered her marriage; but
fhe had been fo long at Lady Edwin's houfe,
after her fon arrived, before he had feen her,
it would, perhaps, have been too late, then,
to have obtained her unfullied hand; and
however abandoned has been the life of a
libertine, let his actions have been branded
with every breach of the laws of honour,
gratitude, or hofpitality, let him have called

led the holy hoft of heaven to witnefs, his perjuries, let beauty, innocence, and virtue, have been his prey, be it remembered, fuch a character, though worn out with every vice to which human nature is liable in its moft depraved ftate, he expects he is yet entitled to the difinterefted affections, the pure and unblemifhed heart of whatever happy woman happens to ftrike his worn-out tafte.

As the fond wifh we are apt in our fanguine expectations to form, leaves us, we are then, while hope and fancy play around the imagination, fond of feizing on the next good thing we look forward to.

Thus, Anna, courted by Edwin, one of the handfomeft young men of the age, if it were poffible fhe had yet retained her virtue, would not, furely, yield to him; her old prejudices yet alive, perhaps, fufpecting, what was truth, that he had helped to deprive her of her friends in Grofvenor-fquare, as well as Somerfet-fhire.

But

But to be a lady, to make her miſtreſs of himſelf and fate, could ſhe, in nature, refuſe that? Yet to beſtow himſelf and fortune on an orphan, a girl nobody knew; were all his intrigues to end in ſo inglorious a union; but then the charming image of Anna decked in jewels, ornamented by dreſs and equipage, rendering him the envy of all the young fellows of the age, aroſe in his idea, and baniſhed from thence every mortifying retroſpect of what had been, in the enchanting hope of what might yet be; and he determined, if he found her uncontaminated, pure, and worthy ſo capital a pieſe of felicity, to offer her his hand.

Madame Frajan was announced in that inſtant; but a day before this viſit from the partner in his iniquity would have been the moſt acceptable thing that could have happened; at preſent it was rather *mal-a-propos*. However ſhe was too deep in his ſecrets to be affronted, ſhe was therefore admitted —Her lengthened face and meaning eyes convinced him there was ſomething to to be told; but curiosity had now little room in a heart totally absorbed in the delightful ideas of possessing the most lovely of women.

Frajan was too full of her errand to observe this change; and having prefaced her story by desiring now to remind him of what she had frequently asserted, that tho' the English woman possessed not that noble frankness which rendered the gallantry of French ladies more conspicuous, they were none of them averse to intrigue:—The demure little Anna, for instance, though she wanted penetration and taste to suffer his Lordship to initiate her into the soft passion, had not been so cruel to Mr. Edwin, by whom she was now actually kept. This intelligence, delivered partly with reproach and partly with spite, found not such credit with Lord Sutton as some other of that lady's invention, with his aid, had done from the family she served.

He knew the last part to be false, as well as many other things laid to the charge of Anna; but the case was now altered, the

K 6 injuries

injuries done to the character of a deferted orphan might not, perhaps, become necessary to clear Lady Sutton; as the blemishes, which would ruin the one, and deprive her of the means of procuring an honest subsistence would be lost in the affluence and dignity of the other. But yet there were some few obligations our heroine owed to the invention of him and his affociate, Madam Frajan, which it would be by no means convenient Anna should be acquainted with, at least while it was out of her power to acknowledge them as they deferved.—But for this confideration, the league betwixt thofe two worthy friends would have been inftantly diffolved, as it had never yet happened that he had fet the leaft regard on any one perfon longer than he could in fome fhape or other make them fubfervient to his intereft, or dropped with the leaft reluctance any one who had done him the laft good office in their power.

His Lordfhip had now no thought of his fair emiffary, but how to caft on her

the

the odium of every injury done Anna by their joint means.

Cooly, therefore, he affured her, fhe had been mifinformed, that he was better acquainted with Anna's fituation and fen-timents, and believed the firft was reput-able, the latter untainted.—The air that accompanied this declaration ftruck poor Frajan dumb; Lord Sutton turned the friend of Anna, then muft he be inevit-ably her enemy, fince if admitted to her converfation, difcoveries muft be made which *fhe* could not ftand the brunt of. However, one confolation remained; fhe had likewife difcoveries in her power, which, on occafion, fhe was determined to make ufe of. Female fpite required this piece of juftice, on a man who had, from the beginning, deceived even her; and his fuffering her to depart without the accuftomed douceur, which fhe al-ways reckoned on as her undoubted per-quifite, contributed not a little to the vindictive fpirit in which fhe left him.

Lord

Lord Sutton, full of his intended pro-
ject, and the happiness he expected to re-
fult from his deep-laid fcheme, paid little regard to the fuddenefs of her exit;
one difficulty now ftruck him, which was,
how to get rid of his two fultanas; the
one in the houfe with him, was a poor,
fpiritlefs, meek, creature, whofe whole
pleafure centered in the children fhe had
by a tender and worthy deceafed hufband;
—his pleafures or purfuits were equally
uninterrupted by her: indeed, in his opinion, fhe was but one degree removed
from ideotifm; he promifed himfelf to
part with her without the leaft trouble or
expence: at prefent, the honefty of her
difpofition, and the œconomy which
(though reduced from very promifing expectations) had always been her practice,
made her a very valuable manager in his
family. Profufion and meannefs are very
nearly allied; nothing that could feed his
pride or vanity, nothing that could contribute to the gratification of his appetite
of any fort, was thought much of by
                                        him;—

him;—but though from a scene of impo-
sition, waste and expence, Mrs. Villers
had established order and regularity, and
consequently his house-keeping bills were
one half reduced, her accounts were sure
to meet a thousand faults, nor even settled without being reminded of the value
of money, of the poverty from which he
had relieved her, and the distress she
must be again exposed to, if deprived
of his protection.

The settled unchangeable countenance
with which those harangues were received,
contributed not a little to confirm his notions of her stupidity; he could, therefore, turn *her* out when it was convenient; but the woman he kept at Bath,
who was the same that on his first return
from India, he had in the parade of his wealth
and oriental consequence, established a
first-rate courtezan, who dared do any
thing she took into her head, and who, by
threats and cunning, had contrived to be
supported in splendour, by a man who
entertained not the least inclination for
her,

her, and indeed who never had any—
How fhould he do with *her?*

One certain plague which attends old
rakes and coquettes, is the mortification
fure to be inflicted at every hint of en-
creafing age; it was a plague particularly
tormenting to Sutton; it was his very
fore place; Charlotte Madden knew every
weak point about him; and the art of
turning this knowledge to her own advantage was what fhe was by no means defici-
ent in. Our hero ftood fo much in awe
of this charming appendage to his ftate,
that though the houfe and eftablifhment
at Bath were elegant and expenfive; and
though the waters of that delightful
place were allowed to be the moft falu-
tary for conftitutions broken by long refidence in a hot climate; it was the place
he was leaft feen at. For this piece of
felf denial he had two excufes, bufinefs
in winter, and indifpofition in fummer;
and provided his charmer had been of the
party, he would have fairly compounded
with ny one, to til the whole at a very
cheap rate off his hands.

His heart recoiled the moment Charlotte came acrofs his memory: had he been going to be united to a modern woman of fafhion, a large jointure and double pin money would have filenced the fcruples of a fafhionable belle, who, contented to lead in her own fet, would not perhaps have been offended at her hufband's miftrefs's claiming the fame advantage as thofe fhe affociated with.

But the purity of the mind of Anna, and the old-fafhioned notions fhe inherited from Mrs. Manfel, would, he well knew, fhrink from fuch an idea; to get rid of Charlotte, therefore, was indifpenfably neceffary; but how, was another thing too difficult to be directly determined upon. Banifhing, therefore, fuch an unpleafant fubject, again he indulged himfelf in contemplating the charms of his future bride, in figuring to himfelf the ferenity of his life with fuch a companion, and in furnifhing his mind with arguments to combat his mifgiving, on account of Edwin.

CHAP

CHAPTER XLIV.

The Difappointment.

NEXT morning carried him to Layton. Dalton and his family were dreffed, in expectation of the honour he did them; but Anna was not of the party; a circumftance that gave him no difquiet, as he was glad of the opportunity to inquire if any thing farther had tranfpired, relating to the fuppofed connection with Edwin.

He was overjoyed to hear from Mrs. Dalton, fhe was convinced, as far as related to Anna, it was totally void of foundation; he only wanted this to induce him to open his intention, which he did, with all the parade and oftentation his heart abounded in, at the fame time making a full difplay of the extreme generofity of his motives, in waving every confideration of birth and fortune, to

make

make himfelf the legal protector of a deftitute young creature, who muft elfe fall
a prey to the wicked intrigues of a libertine age.—The furprize of the Daltons
is not to be defcribed at this declaration,
nor their joy, at the connection they had
an opportunity of forming, by fo eligible
a match for their ward, who would now
amply repay all their kindnefs fhe was fuppofed to receive from their hands:—in the
fulnefs of their hearts they complimented
the noble lord, and they congratulated
each other; his goodnefs they extolled to
the fkies; while the afpiration of their
own hopes feemed to follow his exultation.

When full two hours had been employed, to the mutual fatisfaction of the
vifitor and vifited, his Lordfhip expreffed
his wifh to be admitted to the fight of
his intended bride: fhe had gone out before breakfaft, and was not returned;
her acquaintance was fo fmall in the village; it was eafy to trace it; the maid
was therefore difpatched to Mrs. Wellers',
with Mrs. Dalton's requeft fhe would immediately come home. The girl returned

turned with anſwer, that Miſs Manſel
breakfaſted with Mrs. Wellers, who had
taken her to town in the carriage, but
that they were expected back to dinner:
—Sutton was diſapqointed and angry:
who the d—l is this Wellers, ſaid he,
and why do you ſuffer her to go out
alone?—Dalton ſatisfied him as to the
propriety of her companion, and both
promiſed, till they had the honour of deli-
vering her into his own hands, ſhe never
more ſhould go out of their ſight.—This
promiſe hardly pacified him:—he was
dreſſed, both himſelf and epuipage, to at-
tract all eyes; armed at all points, he had
flattered himſelf he was irreſiſtible; it was,
therefore, with extreme regret, he gave up
the expectation of ſeeing her that day;
yet to wait her return and again ſend for
her, would be opening his addreſſes, which,
notwithſtandnig his great vanity, he had
ſome ſerious fear about—in rather an
awkward way, he was therefore obliged
to poſtpone this weighty affair; and,
charging Dalton with his compliments,
&c. he told him he ſhould write to her

as foon as he got to town:—the carriage
being then ordered to draw to the door,
with half the town round it in full gaze,
affecting an air of humility and good
humour, after bowing to the doffed hats
of the mob, he was drawn off.

During the time his carriage was in
waiting, the young diftiller I have before
mentioned, paffed the houfe; and meeting a neighbour, who had the honour of
mixing medicines for the infirm in that
and the adjacent villages, the diftiller,
ready to burft with the importance of his
own ideas, obferved the extreme elegance
of the vis-a-vis, and, with a fneer, fuppofed Mifs would be for cutting as great
a figure as the Bird of Paradife. The
doctor was a man of good understanding,
and a tolerable fhare of profeffional knowledge; but having met, in his domeftic
circle, fome embaraffment, which called
on the utmoft exertions of induftry to
counteract, he had very little knowledge
of the world, with which Mr. Bibbins
affured him he was perfectly acquainted;
what,

what, therefore, was that gentleman's meaning, when he fpoke of the Bird of Paradife, he could not conceive.

The young gentleman, in pity to his ignorance, told him it was in high life a courtezan; that the girl at the Parfon's was of the fame ftamp, as he himfelf had often feen her in places where he and people of the genteeleft fort reforted; places, indeed, that required drefs, (viewing with no fmall felf-approbation, the pink knee-ftrings that adorned the upper part of his pretty legs, and heels of the fame colour that terminated that lovely part of his charming perfon) befides the money it coft to get into them.

" And how came this lady to conde-
" fcend, then, in the full bloom of youth
" and beauty to leave thofe gay connec-
" tions?" afked the Doctor—" Oh, God!
" how ignorant you are," returned Bib-
" bins, " of life: why, thefe fort of folks
" have all their *ups and downs*—that,
" now, is the Duke of I——'s carriage;
" he vifits her incog. only, till fhe has
" obtained

" obtained a fettlement from a rich Welch
" Squire, who is married and wants to get
" rid of her."

A young man of plain, but genteel, appearance, whofe attention feemed to be
taken with the fame gaudy object, afked
Mr. Bibbins if he was fure he was not
miftaken, as the coronet was not ducal—
Another opportunity now offered for the
difplay of his knowledge of great folks in
the perfon of the ftranger; he anfwered
with an air of pofitive affurance, that he
knew his Grace perfectly well, that he had
great dealings amongft minifters, and *them
there* fort of folks; that the prime minifter
often fent for and confulted both him and
his father on affairs of ftate; and it was
impoffible he could be miftaken in any of
the Lords or Dukes of the court; becaufe
why, he often and often had been there;
and his own uncle, Sir Gilbert Mufhroom,
had been knighted. Proofs like thefe,
were damning ones; indeed they were
unanfwerable, or at leaft unanfwered by
the young. ftranger, whofe involuntary
fighs,

fighs, turned the attention both of the
Doctor and young Bibbins from the equipage at the door to the perfon whofe emotions it vifibly excited.

There was fomething in him that raifed
a good-natured curiofity in the Doctor.
To Bibbins he was a bore; and having
in his remark of the coronet fhewn a fuperior knowledge to the beau, was directly
concluded by him to be a herald-painter
and a low fellow—Now, though in the
practice of that art, if he had by any kind
of means contrived to acquire a fortune,
or, without one, could drefs fo vaftly well
as he, Mr. Bibbins, did; there was nothing that could or ought to have fhocked
his nicety—but the plainnefs of his appearance, a dejected turn of countenance,
and fallen cheeks, were objects that at once
bringing his own appofite perfections in
view, infpired him with fovereign contempt: turning, therefore on his heel,
humming Tally-ho, without any ceremony
he walked off, leaving the doctor and
ftranger ftill in view of Dalton's door, the

latter

latter with fixed attention there, and the former as fixedly obferving him.

Docter Collet, I have faid, was too much engaged in the concerns of his family and patients, to be very converfant in the great world; and, as is the conftant practice in fmall country places, the embarraffments of his domeftic circle had been fo perverfely handled by the goodnatured idlers of the village, that his wife dying of a confumption, he had been fet down as her actual murderer by one half, and (a woman, whofe natural peevifh and refractory difpofition had not only banifhed peace from her own bofom, but her habitation) fanctified, as the very beft creature in the world, by the other.

The Doctor's pride on one hand, and the particularity of his difpofition on the other, always prevented his explanation, which, like Sterne's Yoric, he could have made in his own favour, and had well nigh loft all his female patients, as well as his character, before he dreamed of either being in danger; when, however, he found

the predicament in which he ſtood, two
methods only offered; one was, by going
round the families who had been prejudiced againſt him, and expoſing, not only
the follies but the vices of the dead, and
endeavour to recover his loſt ground;
the other, to retrench the expences of his
houſe, and rely on his unimpeached ſkill
for as much buſineſs as would barely ſupport him, and leave the neighbourhood
to their own opinions; this was the leaſt
trouble, and this he adopted, devoting
all his leiſure to ſtudy and chemical
whims, and encouraging a diſpoſition to
deſpiſe mankind; but as this ſourneſs of
heart was more the effect of habit and neceſſity, than principle or choice, the natural good nature and philanthropy of his
ſoul ſometimes broke out through the
midſt of contracted petulence; and as in
the preſent inſtance, his heart yearned
with good-will to his fellow creatures.

But though he was ſo obdurate to the
calls of curioſity in his own affairs, no perſon living could be more intereſted in thoſe

of

of other people, or take greater pains to
make himfelf acquainted with the caufes
as well as effects of every occurrence in
and about his own village; nor was he,
to do him juftice, a bit fparing of the intelligence fo induftrioufly procured; dif-
penfing liberally at one houfe all that occurred at another, fometimes feafoned
with a little of the acrimony of his own
feelings, and that without the leaft intention of injuring any individual, but merely
to indulge himfelf in the exhibition of his
talents, and for *thofe* he happily entertained a very great refpect; really unconfcious, though fo great a fufferer in
his own character, of the mifchief his
eternal goffip produced, he was the firft
to condemn the practice he adopted, and
as ready to contradict any report, though
circulated by himfelf, when convinced
of its falfity, as to enforce its credit,
when fure of its being true.

What could he poffibly figh for? What
could the girl be to him? he would give
the world to know—but curiofity, power-

ful

ful as was its influence on the mind of Dr. Collet, was ever vanquished by humanity; a sudden paleness which overspread the face of the stranger, the evident distress of his looks, and his interesting appearance, altogether excited his attention and respect; he intreated him to go home with him to his house, which was within sight—the offer was accepted with a polite freedom, and a few moments served to settle a very good understanding between the doctor and his new acquaintance, who acknowledged that it was of the utmost importance to him to know every particular concerning Anna Manfel. A firm promise in return was given by Collet, to make it his business to inform him of all he could learn; gratifying at once, by their league, his two favourite, though contradictory, pursuits, curiosity and good nature; on which errand he immediately fallied out.

CHAP.

CHAPTER XLV.

The Morning Visit.

WITH Dalton Collet had no acquaintance; that good man had a mortal aver-
fion to phyfical bills, nor would ever fuffer one to be incurred in his family: but
he had heard of Bently's affair, and Bibbins' account of Anna was a confirmation
that the report then fpread was but too
true; however, he was refolved to be
fomething better informed, if poffible,
and as he had the honour of attending
the family of Mr. Juftice Strap, he took
occafion to call with a How d'ye? on his
lady.

There he met, on a fimilar vifit to the
Mifs Straps, Mifs Bibbins, the young
lady I have before introduced as a perfon perfectly acquainted with the bad

character

character of our heroine—Doctor Collet
was nobody; he, therefore, was no inter-
ruption to that young lady's volubility,
who continued her account of a dreſs
which ſeemed to have made no ſmall diſ-
turbance in her ideas.

" The flounce, if you will believe me,
" ma'am, was near half a yard deep, of
" the fineſt corded muſlin, put on as
" thick as poſſible—the train, though
" looped up, I am ſure was of a mon-
" ſtrous length; why, dear me, mamma
" ſays it is not a little pays for thoſe
" things; then, ma'am, her linen is ſo
" fine—and it is a ſhame to ſee the lace
" ſhe wears—beſides ſhe certainly paints."
—" That is very evident," anſwered the
eldeſt Miſs Strap—" I am aſtoniſhed Mrs.
" Wellers can take up with ſuch trum-
" pery."—" Oh, as to that, my dear,"
anſwered Mrs. Strap, " it is eaſy accoun-
" ted for; Mrs. Wellers, you know,
" takes on her to lead us all—and per-
" haps ſhe may hope to introduce this
" minx by way of ſhewing her power;

" some folks who are very well them-
" selves, may fancy what they please,
" but there are folks whose characters
" are of consequence."

" Certainly, ma'am," said Miss Bibbins, " that is what my mamma says;
" and besides, as she says, the thing is
" past doubt; for how could such a girl
" as that wear about in her common
" dress, things that are so expensive and
" out of character for her; besides, her
" affectation of modesty, shunning the
" eyes of the men, nothing is easier, than
" to see that it is all a farce—I have no
" patience with such creatures."

" This," replied Mrs. Strap, is one
" of the blessed effects of Mr. Thornhill's
" establishing his meeting here; I assure
" you, I think it very hard the Miss
" Straps, and you, Miss Bibbins, and
" the other young ladies of the place,
" cannot walk out without being shocked
" by the sight of a kept woman."

Collet had sat with some degree of im-
patience, in hope of edging in a word, by
way of gaining the intelligence he sought

after,

after, till the laft part of the converfation;
when underftanding, what he had at firft
no fufpicion of, that Mifs Manfel was the
fubject of it, he became not only attentive,
but, by juft afking a queftion now and
then, when a paufe of the fair declaimers
would fuffer him, he learned that Mifs
Manfel was a vile young woman; that fhe
had feduced the affections of the lady's
fon fhe ferved, though fhe then knew he
was under engagement to be married to
a young heirefs of fafhion; that he had
turned her off; and that fhe was now
making ufe of every artifice to procure a
fettlement from him, by threatening to
difclofe the affair to his lady; and that
fhe was privately vifited by more than
one gentleman *now*, though they could
not pofitively think what attractions fhe
had:—but men, Mifs Bibbins obferved,
had very ftrange taftes.

. So much for the account at the wor-
fhipful Mr. Straps', who corroborated the
whole by reciting, in his own way, the
adventure of the horfewhip, making no
fecret of the gentleman's name, though
he

he had pledged his word it fhould not be known. Having thus fucceeded beyond his expectations, Collet took his leave.

The ladies he parted from affured him of the truth of every tittle he had heard; but there was one circumftance weighed againft all they could fay about our heroine, and that was, the favours fhewn her by Mrs. Wellers; that lady, by the uprightnefs of her own character, and the benevolence of her fentiments, had actually arrived at the happy perfection of keeping in awe her enemies, as well as being adored by her friends, and univerfally refpected by people whofe underftanding and principles rendered their refpect of value: to couple infamy and Mrs. Wellers together, was a union which could never ftrike Collet; he knew and revered her; and it was not in the power of Juftice Strap, his amiable wife, his charming daughters, or their good friend Mifs Bibbins, to convince him Anna Manfel was a bad woman, when the next breath, added fhe was at the Hill: he hefitated, as he came out of Mr. Strap's gates, whether he could return to his new friend, or by walking, or rather hobbling, being much afflicted with the gout, to Mrs. Wellers', where he might reasonably hope to hear some extenuation of the facts so roundly asserted at Justice Strap's.

When Collet did any thing without consideration, it often appeared, and perhaps sometimes was, from a sudden splenetic fit which looked too like ill-nature; but if he took a moment's thought, if he hesitated, let the trouble, expence, or fatigue, be ever so great, provided it was not in his own concern, good nature, justice, and humanity were sure to conquer;—and he was creeping up the green to Hill-house, before he had suffered a second thought to obtrude, besides that pleasing one, inspired with a love of truth. This was not one of Anna's lucky days: Mrs. Wellers, as I before said, had taken her to town; and the disappointment reminded Collet of his gout; he had all the way to walk back, and, what was worse, no better for the journey, which in the return was painful and fatiguing. He
found

found the ftranger impatiently waiting for him, and briefly related all he had heard; not however fuffering the fretful fit, then on him, to hinder his likewife telling his own more favourable thoughts.

My reader will perhaps have anticipated the difcovery I am going to make of the inquifitive ftranger: it was indeed Charles Herbert, who, after making ten thoufand refolutions to forget the owner of the breaft bow, could think of nothing elfe; and who broke, in his excurfion to Layton, as many vows he had made never to inquire after her; and who now felt that, worthlefs, and even abandoned, as he had had every reafon to believe Anna, it was not in his nature to ceafe loving her.

Collet, gouty, poor, and a humourift, was at that very time a lover; not a defpairing one, for the objeét of his affections was far from bein out of the reach of his purfuit; not a fuccefsful one, for his diffidence in his own merits was unconquerable; nor did he guard the fecret of his paffion with more care from

L 6   the

the ridicule of his acquaintance, than from the knowledge of *her* who infpired it; but he was a lover, and confequently very eafily faw the fituation of Herbert.

Glad of any difcovery, and very much pleafed with his new friend, he readily promifed to have a conftant eye on Anna, and to communicate to him every thing that occurred concerning her; they parted with mutual profeffions of friendfhip. Herbert, though his heart was burfting with love and defpair, when he left Layton, felt a gleam of confolation from Collet's promifed correfpondence.

CHAP.

CHAPTER XLVI.

A second Plan for female Education.

ANNA's interest in the affection of the worthy woman, to whose advice she wisely resolved to submit herself, was hourly increasing: she had been received at the Hill with that open friendship which not only encourages, but demands our confidence; she therefore found no difficulty from the innate modesty of her sentiments, when so kindly encouraged, but told Mrs. Wellers, without the least reserve, her whole history, not concealing a single event which presented itself to her recollection, excepting only the feelings of her heart towards young Herbert.

The many changes in the life of so young a creature; the enemies she had so undeservedly met; her destitute infancy, and

present

prefent uncomfortable fituation, were of
many arguments in favour of the partiality
Mrs. Wellers felt for her, that fhe promifed not only to confider her affairs, but
give her every affiftance and advice in her
power; and, *a propos*, faid fhe, I am going
to town this morning, and will take you
to my daughter's, where we will confult
what can be done for fo amiable a girl.

Anna's gratitude was not given to words
the tears which Mrs. Wellers affection-
ately wiped off, fpoke their own language,
and they both went to town in Mrs.
Wellers' coach.

Young Mrs. Wellers was, I have before
faid, a plain, good woman; the large fortune fhe had brought her hufband intitled
her to every indulgence a prudent woman
could defire. She was devoted to her
children, and her pride was that of making
them (they were all girls) the moft accomplifhed women of the age. She was herfelf the only daughter of a very covetuous
rich old man, to whofe penury it was owing that his daughter regretted perpetually

ally her confined education:—Not one of
the accompliſhments ſhe beheld in other
ladies of her rank in the world had been
taught her; but from the moment ſhe became a mother, ſhe was reſolved her children ſhould profit by her misfortune—and
the whole of her time was dedicated to
the watching over the education of her
daughters.

Unread and unexperienced, it will not
be wondered if this diſpoſition, amiable as
it was, carried her into the oppoſite extreme: her avarice of inſtruction for them
was viſible in all her furniture and apartments; globes, books, frames, muſical
inſtruments, ſtocks, collars, and ſwings,
were not confined to one or two rooms,
her houſe was a ſeminary of female learning; and the humble rap at the door all
the morning, announced the arrival of the
different inſtructors. The dancing ſtep
ſometimes preceded the diſmiſſion of the
back ſtring, and they knew the *aw* and *bè*
of the French long before they had an
idea of the Engliſh alphabet.

Without

Without either ear or voice Mrs. Wellers, determined her daughters should be proficients in music: and with capacities which rendered it difficult for them to receive an idea of the four quarters of the globe, they were expected to excel in geographical knowledge. Work, indeed, was out of her system: embroidery, Quadrille baskets, cutting of paper, and other trifles of a trifling age, indeed, were the only employments it was necessary should engage their attention, but not even of them did she make any point.

Her mother-in-law saw with the eyes of indulgence the excess to which this passion of her daughter carried her; she was most respectfully attended to on every other subject, but her remonstrances were so ill received on this, that she prudently declined repeating them; and rather sought to dress in an amiable light, what to herself appeared a weakness in her daughter.

The accomplishments and abilities of Anna struck in a particular manner, as capable of being of more real advantage to

her

her grand children, than the laboured inftructions of the different mafters who attended them; at leaft they would be more
likely to catch the manners of a gentlewo-
man from her (whofe native grace and politenefs fpoke her fit to adorn any rank)
than the hired foreign fervants about them.
There was but óne difficulty that fhe forefaw would be a hard one to furmount;
which was, her knowing fo little of the
French language—it was therefore that
fhe did not explain her intentions in taking her to town.

When they arrived in Charter-houfe-
fquare, Mrs. Wellers immediately afcended
to the third floor, which was entirely devoted to the young ladies: the mafters and
attendants, mother and daughters, were
all engaged. In one room the mufic mafter
was giving his inftructions; in another
the globes were difplayed; in the third a
pretty little girl was practifing a *pas feul*;
and in a large detached clófet, another
(overlooked by mamma) was attempting
a land-

a landſcape, attended by a French governeſs and two maids of the ſame nation.

Grandmamma's arrival immediately
made a little holiday—the children hung
round her, while their mamma was likewiſe expreſſing the pleaſure this viſit gave
her. The two ladies ſoon retired, leaving
Auna much amuſed and ſurpriſed at a
ſight ſo new; ſhe ſat down to the harpſi-
chord with that avidity and pleaſure a
lover of muſic, who has long been deprived of an inſtrument, only can conceive. Her execution and taſte, I have
before ſaid, were beyond her inſtručtions.
The maſter, who was not yet gone, paid
her many compliments on her performance; and ſhe was ſo delighted with the
opportunity of reſuming her favourite
amuſement, that the ladies, who were an
hour abſent, when they returned found her
loſt in her own harmony.

The intermediate time had been ſpent
by the benevolent Mrs. Wellers in introducing to her ſon and daughter in the
                                    moſt

moſt favourable and amiable light the orphan ſhe had promiſed to befriend.

Mr. Wellers was a plain, honeſt, moral man, whoſe feelings were regulated by his ideas of juſtice; the integrity of his dealings were univerſally known, but he was not more regular in his books and accounts than in his inclinations: He behaved with friendſhip and affection to his wife, and gave his whole time and attention to the intereſt of his family:—increaſing his fortune for their advantage, he reckoned all the fondneſs incumbent in a father.

What warmth there was about him was more particularly towards his parents—whoſe generoſity in parting with their all for his eſtabliſhment, was by him called confidence in his credit: and that is a ſort of obligation men of buſineſs never forget. One regular mode of life carried him thro' the year. At one hour you was ſure to find him at breakfaſt, at the Bank, at Change, and at dinner. The evening he gave to his wife, and Sunday to his parents. But it was equally out of the nature of
things

things to work him up to an act of benevolence, or prevail on him to be guilty
of one of oppreffion. His fenfibility
neither hurt his own peace, or affected
that of other people. His mother's example, as far as it taught him rigid probity, had its effect, but the foftnefs and humanity, the warmth of friendfhip, and the
entire love of virtue which foftened her
whole foul, fhe had not the happinefs to
fee actuate the fentiments of her fon.

With an attention his refpect for her
had enforced, he heard her commendation
of Anna; and when his wife, charmed at
his mother's account of her abilities, though
fenfibly mortified at her deficiency in the
language fo neceffary for her daughters,
afked his approbation of her being taken
as governefs into the houfe, in his ufual
ftile he gave way to their opinions; flightly
obferving, the world was fo deceitful, he
fuppofed Mrs. Wellers would inform herfelf of the truth of the ftory fhe had been
repeating. She had, fhe faid, no kind of
doubt of the leaft tittle; but however, as
character

character to be sure should be the first recommendation in the situation to which she proposed placing her young friend, she was sure Anna would object to no inquiries proper to be made at Lady Edwin's.

Things being in this happy train for our heroine, Mrs. Wellers returned with her to Layton without having said any thing of her plan till they were returning in the carriage from town, when she explained the nature of the service she meant to do her: at the same time adding, if the children were happy enough to engage her affection, as well as care, the obligation would be all on their side, since she was sure her example and society would be to them of the most serious advantage.

Anna was overwhelmed with gratitude —but diffident of her abilities to undertake what to her appeared a talk of such consequence, restrained the lively and animated expressions of it which filled her gentle bosom, she frankly confessed doubts of herself; those doubts were the surest proofs of her capability; and the good-natured Mrs. Wellers only found the stronger

reasons

reasons to congratulate herself on such an acquisition. With respect to the inquiries necessary to be made in Grosvenor-square, it was a matter of joy, conscious of the purity of her conduct; and having told her friend every circumstance respecting young Edwin, and the conclusions made upon it by the Daltons, she had nothing to fear; on the contrary, it would explain a matter that had hitherto been so deep a mystery, and perhaps once more enable her to see her dear Miss Herbert. She might yet know how fate would dispose of her brother—she therefore not only consented with alacrity, but urged Mrs. Wellers to go the next day. Her desires were too agreeable to that lady's own wish not to be complied with. When they alighted at the Hill they were told of Mrs. Dalton's message; and Anna, fearing she might be indisposed, begged leave to go home directly; which, however, she was not permitted to do till evening.

END OF THE SECOND VOLUME.